ISLAND HEAT

DEEP WATER OCTOPUS

A. C. Stone & D. C. Stone

Grosvenor House
Publishing Limited

This book is published by
Grosvenor House Publishing Ltd
Link House
140 The Broadway, Tolworth, Surrey, KT6 7HT.
www.grosvenorhousepublishing.co.uk

This book is a work of fiction. Any resemblance to
people or events, past or present, is purely coincidental.

A CIP record for this book
is available from the British Library

ISBN 978-1-80381-287-8
eBook ISBN 978-1-80381-288-5

In society's quest for unity, equality, and inclusiveness, they have created disunity, inequality, and exclusiveness. For when you start stripping away things like gender, race, colour, age, and physical appearances, and start replacing words with generic words, or trying to dictate words, that can, and can't be said in order not to cause offence, then you find people who feel as though they are unseen, and unheard. You in effect create a society of faceless people.

Yet it is in our differences that make us unique, and it's our uniqueness that should be celebrated, and uplifted. It is our differences that brings beauty into the world.

Boooooom

Trae jolted upright in bed; his heart thumped loudly, as he scrambled underneath the bed. *What the hell was that?* He waited for a few minutes before he edged his way back out. He sniffed the air as he put his slippers on. *Smoke!*

He shivered as a gust of wind blew across his body. *What the?* The light from the streetlight outside his bedroom window, shone through the ripped curtain, and reflected off broken pieces of glass, that lay strewn across the floor. The sound of sirens echoed in the room. As the emergency vehicles drew closer; their blue and red lights lit up the room like a disco.

Trae looked out of the window, as he heard voices yelling at each other. *My car!* He pulled his dressing gown on as he ran out of the unit, outside, to where the firefighters were finishing hosing down the burnt remains. 'My car!'

'Is no more' the chief firefighter patted Trae on the back. 'Cheer up, we saved the unit.'

'I had one payment left.' Trae walked slowly back into his unit, occasionally stopping, and turning, to look at the smouldering wreck. *One payment, and she would've been mine.* He sighed and shut the front door.

Stop it. I'm being transferred. It's all good. He smiled as he changed into his uniform. *This next move is going to be awesome. No more unsettled weather. The island was a pleasant twenty-eight degrees, all year round, or so General Melon had said.*

Trae started to sweep up the broken glass, as the rays from the sun that had started to rise glittered off the shards. He was glad that the room was barren. Now that his belongings were gone, only the essentials remained, his bed, and a cupboard, which was good, as it meant, that he didn't have to worry about finding glass bits in his belongings.

He finished sweeping the glass into a pile. *That will have to be picked up when they clean the place.* He walked over to the bedroom door, and shut it, so that he could look in the mirror that was attached to the back of the door. He twisted to the left, and then to the right, making sure that every crease of his uniform was perfectly done, just as he had been taught, when he first joined the army, much to his parent's horror.

Those free, peace-loving hippies. His phone rang. *Not answering it* he let it go to the answering machine. 'Moonbeam' he cringed when he heard his father's voice say his birth name 'your mother and I are so worried about you. We don't like the idea of you transferring yet again.'

And I hate the name you gave me. He ran his hand over his shaven head. Small spikes of black hair had started to grow again. I *really should get my hair shaved again.* Perfection, everything had to be done to perfection, or should've been done to perfection. It was a shame that people didn't appreciate the order that was instilled in the army or tried to be. They didn't understand his need for order, or the respect that he was looking for.

2

Trae sighed. *The army has certainly changed since I joined. Maybe it was because there had been no major wars, well, apart from a few incidents, with some medical faction; the years had been pretty calm, but now, things were finally looking up. Yep – a new job, a new base, a new beginning, and a new chance for some respect. Finally, things are looking up.*

He straightened his tie for the umpteenth time and wandered around the empty unit. A momentary touch of sadness entered him, at the thought of leaving the place, that he had called home for the last eight years.

The barracks were great, for the few months of the year when they trained, but he did prefer his unit, where he could be alone, and away from his fellow soldiers. A shiver ran down his back. How the last lot even enlisted, he had no idea. Some of them he was sure were certifiable.

'Hang on' he called out, as someone knocked on the door. He took a final look in the mirror. *Yep, I'm looking pretty sharp today.* He opened the door, and saluted the cadet, that was standing there, with his hand already raised to salute Trae.

'Here, let me, sir' the cadet took the suitcase, that Trae had picked up.

This is going to be a good day. He locked the door of his unit and followed the cadet to the car. He sat in the back seat, as the cadet put his suitcase in the boot. The sadness that he had felt lessened, as the excitement of what lay ahead, filled its place. This was the beginning of a new adventure. He was sure that he had made the right decision.

'Are you ready, sir?' the driver slowly began to drive forward.

Too bad, if he wasn't but he was ready, he was very ready. 'Yes, yes I am thank you.' *This was it*. The car slowly picked up more speed. *No turning back; this is a new beginning, and about time.* Alone with his thoughts, his mind drifted back to the meeting he had yesterday, in General Melon's office.

'Did you get the file that was sent to you?' General Melon started to sift through the piles of paperwork on his table. He started to throw some of the files on the floor 'Because I can't find it at the moment.'

'Yes, I did.' Trae shuddered at the mess the general was making, and wondered how anyone so disorganised, could become a general.

General Melon scratched his head. 'I know what you're thinking, Trae.'

I seriously doubt that.

'You think that this office is a mess.' General Melon spun his chair around, so that he could pick up a pile of files, off the small filing cabinet that was behind him. He spun around, and put them on the table, in front of him. 'I know your penchant for order. I can see it on your face: you think this office is a mess.'

Trae looked around the office. Everything was in disarray. Files were piled high on General Melon's desk; piles of files littered the floor, and the tops of the filing cabinets in his office. The only thing that wasn't out of place was a replica of one of the planes used in the war, although which one he wasn't sure, was hanging from the roof. 'That would be rather presumptuous of me, sir.'

'This is not a mess.' General Melon threw a file on the floor 'This is organised chaos. I know where everything is. Well, at least in the general direction.'

Trae didn't say a word as the general kept rambling. He wondered how old the general was. The general's voice sounded so ancient, but no one, that Trae had talked to, could remember when the general first arrived. All they knew was that it was a long time ago. The general just seemed to always be there; maybe it was his fitness regime that kept him so fit.

'Well, what did you think?'

'Are you serious?' Trae's voice came out a little higher than he had hoped. He relaxed for a few moments before speaking again. 'That place looks amazing. Are you sure you sent me the right file?'

'Ah, there you are.' General Melon picked up a file and handed it to Trae. The photos that were in it fell out as Trae took hold of the file. 'You tell me.'

Trae looked at the photos. They were all there, the same pictures that were in the email. He stared at one of the photos that showed an island. It seemed so idyllic, so peaceful, the white sand, and the palm trees. He closed his eyes, and pictured himself, sitting on a deckchair on the beach, sipping an iced tea, with the evening breeze blowing gently over him.

He sighed, opened his eyes, and read the description of the island. Population: 4669, Temperature: average 28 degrees all year, Area mass 2205 kilometres square. Access: there is a landing strip for planes, or a jetty for boats to dock at. The island has one main road with other access roads to get to the various buildings, and dwellings, surrounded by white sand, many palm trees, and other native vegetation.

Roads and housing have been kept to a minimum to ensure the Eco system is not destroyed. Animals: Apart from a rare species of owl, there are no animals on the island, and none are allowed.

A smile grew on his face as he looked at the other photos. The shopping centre, the park – oh, that looked so nice with its green grass, and a fountain, of what strangely looked like an octopus, seemed to be in the middle, with a walkway that meandered its way through the park.

Then there were the banks, pizza places and a doughnut shop, a bowling alley, the Olympic sized swimming pool, and the barracks. It was all there, it seemed, as though every convenience that was possible, had been thought off, and was there. *I really like those barracks. They look so clean, and neat. Everything about the island looks perfect. The people must be awesome to work with. Unlike the idiots and lunatics, that I have to deal with, in my current unit. Especially Peter.*

A cold shiver ran down Trae's back. *That guy thought that he was a motorbike. All day, every day was the same. Peter would run around as though he was a motorbike. His arms were outstretched behind him; his hands were continuing to move as though he were being revved up. And the noises Peter made. He was good at sounding like a motorbike. And the rest of the crew, always trying to ride Peter.*

And, it was funny, for the first week or two, but after three months it was getting scary. It was obvious the guy was insane, but General Melon had said that the army was now progressive. So much so that no one was turned away for their beliefs, even if they did believe they were a motorcycle.

He was so thankful that he had his unit to escape to, but he dreaded returning to the barracks, especially, if his services as a medic were called upon. Trae still couldn't believe it the day, they called him to the barracks, because Peter had somehow run out of fuel.

Trae couldn't believe what was said when he answered the phone. He had to ask 'What?' several times. Even when he told them that it was impossible for Peter to run out of fuel, they wouldn't listen, and insisted that it was true.

He wondered what they were on, but when he arrived at the barracks, they all seemed quite sane, and not under the influence of anything, but they wanted to help Peter. That was the final straw – watching someone put a funnel in Peter's mouth and tipping leaded petrol down it to refuel him, instead of sending him to a hospital.

That was when he started to request a transfer. He liked order, but he liked sanity – his sanity more. And on this island, everything all looked new, and well cared for. There seemed to be every convenience that a person could want. 'It looks fantastic' Trae handed the photos back *and sane*.

'Great.' General Melon pulled out a piece of paper and signed it. 'Because your whinging, I mean, your request for a transfer has been approved. 'But Trae, this is the last time. This is the only unit that wants you.' He handed Trae the paper. 'Just sign at the bottom of the transfer request, and the confidentiality clause, and it's done.'

Absolutely Trae signed the paperwork so fast that he didn't bother to read the confidentiality clause. He'd seen enough of them that he knew the gist, although as he skimmed across the page, he did see something about not taking photos, but he didn't care. He was being transferred. He was out of there.

'So, exactly where am I going?' Trae handed General Melon the papers he had just signed.

'That's top-secret information. What I can tell you is that your med skills will be used. Oh boy, will they be used. Heh, heh, heh, I mean all you need to know right now, is that we'll send a truck to pick up your belongings, and a car will take you to the transport that has been arranged, to take you to the island.' General Melon stood up, his six-foot five frame easily dwarfing Trae's five foot ten and held out his hand for Trae to shake. 'I can't wait for you to meet the Brigadier. He's, um, unique.'

A jolt knocked Trae out of his reverie. 'Sorry about the speed bump' the driver apologised 'we're nearly at the docking point.'

Trae looked out of the car window. *Oh, I'm at the port – must be catching a ship to the island. Wow,* he saw they were heading towards one of the newly built destroyers. *I've always wanted to go on one of those. They had the latest computer technology available and could transport a huge array of weaponry. Things were looking up. Hang on. What?* Confused, Trae watched as the car passed by the destroyer. *But, but* Trae twisted himself around, and saw the destroyer getting smaller as they drove further along the docks.

The car finally pulled to a stop. 'Here you go, Sir.'

'Where's the boat?' Trae opened the car door, confused at where he was 'shouldn't you have stopped where the war ship was.'

'I don't know, I just drive, but the group you're travelling with is standing over there, waiting for you.'

Trae pulled his suitcase out of the boot, and slammed it shut. He walked over to the group and saluted the lieutenant. The lieutenant's mirrored sunglasses caught the rays of the afternoon sun, and momentarily blinded

Trae. 'Now that we are all here' the lieutenant saluted Trae, who had already raised his hand, to salute the lieutenant. 'It's time to board your vessel.'

Vessel, what vessel? Trae heard a groan and looked in the direction of the noise. *What the ... is that someone unconscious on the ground.* He hurried over to where he saw a man lying on the ground where the groups baggage was sitting. He hadn't seen him when he first arrived because of the brightness of the sun. 'Is he alright?' Trae addressed the lieutenant.

'He's been sedated for the trip' the lieutenant replied, as he took off his sunglasses, and wiped the lenses.

'He's coming to!' one of the soldiers yelled.

'Hold him down' the lieutenant, reached into a bag that sat at his feet, and pulled out a tranquilliser gun.

'Wait' Trae stood in front of the man that was slowly stirring 'what are you doing?' '

'Colonel, get out of the way.'

'You can't shoot him' Trae said.

'He's getting up' one of the soldiers called out.

'Stand aside, colonel' the lieutenant warned as he raised the gun to fire 'that is an order.'

'Lieu-' *Oh, he means it* Trae leapt out of the way, just seconds before the lieutenant pulled the trigger.

'Bullseye' the lieutenant laughed as the man slumped back to the ground 'that should keep him quiet until you lot reach the island. Now get aboard' the lieutenant put the gun back in the bag.

'Hey, what are you doing?' Trae yelled as the men rolled the unconscious man over the edge of the wharf. He looked over the edge, and saw he landed on a barge.

'Don't worry about him' one of the men climbed over the edge, and started to climb down the rope ladder that was attached to the dock 'he doesn't feel a thing.'

Were they serious? Trae looked at the barge. *Oh boy! This thing looks like something from the ark.* Trae looked at the helicopter that was sitting in the middle of the barge. *This looks like one of those old wooden fuelling barges I read about, when I studied history at school. But that helicopter, that looks like something out of the museum.*

Trae threw his suitcase onto the deck and climbed down the ladder. *Surely this must be a test. It was the only logical explanation. Yes, that was it, wasn't it?* He jumped onto the deck, the boards creaking under his weight, when he landed.

'I can't believe they, made us climb a rope ladder' Trae spoke to no one in particular. He shook his head as he watched his suitcase being put aboard the helicopter.

'That's nothing.' One of the soldiers said, 'this was designed by a certain engineer of ours; I'm surprised the thing floats.'

This was designed by an engineer. Trae looked around *An engineer! In what?* Trae sighed as they cast off. *Did General Melon even know about this? Well, as soon as we reach the island, I'm going to send in an incident report, to General Melon, to make sure that this never happened again. What were they thinking?*

The barge creaked, and groaned as it rolled up, and down with the waves. *Oh man, this thing sounds like it's on its last legs.* Up and down, up and down, the men were starting to look a little green. Sea sickness: Trae understood it only too well, even he, had trouble keeping his insides in.

He found a spot to lie down on the deck, and let himself, roll with the barge. It was an old trick that he had learnt from some seafarers, several years before. He didn't believe it when he was first told about it, until he tried it out, and was surprised at how much it helped.

He tried to tell the others, that if they lied on the deck and rolled with the barge, the seasickness would go, but they wouldn't listen. They were more content to lean over the side, and throw up, rather than listen to him.

They were all looking forward to getting off this floating wreck, but hour after hour, it kept plodding along, as it rose and fell with the waves. The darkness of night enveloped them, the silence broken by the sounds of the men, who kept throwing up. Trae listened to the men all night, amazed that they had anything left to vomit up. But continue they did, until the morning broke.

'Well, aren't you a sorry, looking bunch!' The lieutenant had come out of one of the cabins that was on the barge, and stood staring at the men, most of who had now collapsed, exhausted from their vomiting marathon. He took his sunglasses out of his pocket and put them on. 'I hope you lot can hold your guts in, long enough to go on a helicopter ride.'

'You want us to go in that thing?' Trae shuddered visibly. *Surely this was a dream. It had to be. No, this was worse than a dream. When am I going to wake up from this nightmare?*

'Yes, it should make it to the island' the lieutenant signalled one of the crew, who went to the helicopter, and tried to start it. 'He should get it going soon.'

'What if I decide I don't want to go?' Trae baulked at the thought of getting on the helicopter.

'Well, that could be a problem, colonel. We're sinking this barge as soon as you lot get off.'

'What? Why are we sinking it?'

'Well, Colonel Trae, there's a few too many design flaws with it, if you must know.'

'So, you are coming with us?' Trae inquired, his moment of relief was short lived, as he heard the lieutenant laugh.

'Are you crazy, colonel? No, I'm returning to the mainland.' The lieutenant pointed out to sea. 'In fact, if you look over there, you can see my ride heading this way.'

In the distance Trae could make out a warship coming towards them. 'Sir, can I come back with you?'

'No. You have the choice of going to the island, or staying on the barge, which we're going to blow up.'

'That's not fair, sir.'

'Now, colonel, you knew this was a one-way ticket.'

'What? No, I didn't.'

'Oh.' The lieutenant shrugged 'You do now.'

Some choice Trae looked at the others who had boarded the helicopter. Sighing he turned and made his way to the last seat that was vacant. *There was no turning back, but man this thing doesn't sound safe. I hope the island isn't too far away; I'm sure I saw some wisps of black smoke coming from the rotor blades when they started to turn.*

The thumping of the blades echoed in the cabin. Trae rubbed his forehead with one hand and looked at his watch. It had been three hours since they left the barge. No wonder he had a headache.

He wondered how much longer the trip would be, as he looked down at the ocean below. If he didn't have such a massive headache, he would probably have enjoyed, looking at the depth of blue that the water wore.

The helicopter started to drop altitude. *Great, we must be nearing our destination. Either that, or the helicopter is going to crash, and we'll be swimming to our destination. But the helicopter seemed to be holding out okay. No, we must be nearing our destination.*

He leaned out of the doorway to see if he could see anything. A strip of white seemed out of place amongst the blue of the ocean, but there it was. The island – they were nearly there.

And, yes, he could just make out green blobs. *They have to be the tops of the palm trees; oh, that looks so nice, they almost seemed to be beckoning them to land.*

The island came into full view as they approached the landing strip. Sandy beach lay on either side of the landing strip. It was so nice, so white, so like the photos that he had seen, he looked forward to landing, and finally getting off the helicopter. A groan interrupted his thoughts. He looked over at the unconscious man who had started to stir.

'Oh, no, not now' one of the soldiers muttered. Trae looked at the other him, and then at the rest of the crew, *that's odd, why do they look so scared.*

Whoa, what was that? An object flew past Trae. Instinctively he reacted and kicked out at it. His intention to kick it out – a failure – as his foot connected, and booted it, into the front with the pilot. A deafening explosion blew out the front of the helicopter, taking the pilot with it, and sending the rest, plummeting to the ground.

Screams echoed in the air, as they held on tight. Trae tried to grab one of them as he fell out, but Trae couldn't keep his grip, and he watched the soldier fall to his death. *This is it! We're all going to die!*

The sound of metal crunching, echoed in Trae's head, the acrid smell of smoke from something burning, penetrated his nostrils. He opened his eyes. *I'm still alive. How?* Trae realised that he had to get out quickly before the fire took hold. A moan alerted him that someone else survived. He crawled over the wreckage to where the moan had come from.

Trae helped the man to his feet, put his arm around the man's shoulders, to help support him, and walked towards a minibus that appeared to be waiting for them. Every step, Trae took, sent an agonising spurt of pain through him. *Ow, I must've broken something.*

The driver of the minibus ran towards him. 'Here, let me help you' the driver urged as he stood on the other side of the injured man, as a few more small explosions echoed around them.

'You take him.' Trae relaxed his grip 'I'll go see if someone else survived.' *What was going on? What were those explosions?*

'It's too late for that. Hurry, get in!'

'No. I ...' Trae turned and looked at the wreckage. The flames had now surrounded the crash site, and were increasing, in their ferocity. *I can't do anything to save anyone.* He limped badly as he followed the driver to the minibus and helped to put the injured man inside.

Trae had barely seated himself when the driver took off. They hadn't got far when a huge explosion echoed in the air. He knew the helicopter had finally blown up. Sirens echoed as fire engines sped passed them, heading towards the burning wreckage.

Better late than never, I guess. He looked at his uniform now torn and shredded. He caught a glimpse of his face in the window. There was a lot of blood, but he was sure that it wasn't serious. He sat back and watched the buildings pass by, as the bus made its way to the base.

People seemed so happy, as they went about their business. There was a calmness that belied his arrival. *The place looked so much like the photos – so peaceful, so idyllic, everything in order; it was so nice and new.* He looked out of the window on the opposite side to where he was sitting and saw the shopping centre as they passed by.

He looked back out of the window near him and saw the park. Trae looked at how green the grass was. It was too green, and perfectly manicured, separated only by the cement walking path that wound its way through. *Maybe it was that – fake grass. But still, it looked so serene and peaceful.*

There were children playing in the park. Many were gathered around the playground. Some children were being pushed on the swings by their parents, others were laughing, as they chased each other around the trees. And in the middle of the park, he could just make out a fountain. *Happiness, laughter and yet my arrival was so bizarre.*

'Shouldn't we stop here?' Trae looked at the hospital as the minibus drove passed.

'We could, but there's a fully equipped section at the base.' The driver changed gears and headed out of the town centre 'Besides they like all injuries that the soldiers suffer, to be treated at the base.'

'I would've thought any hospital would do.'

The driver shrugged 'The rules are different here on the island. You might want to remember that.'

Tree after tree, along what seemed to be an endless road flashed by; it seemed like forever that the bus kept driving. Trae looked at his watch. It hadn't changed time since he had landed. He took off his watch and shook it – *I must've broken it in the crash*. Trae put the watch in what was left of his jacket pocket.

The journey seemed so long, but Trae was sure only an hour at the most had gone by. *How odd* Trae looked at the sign as the bus drove by. 'Quicksand Valley' *why on earth was it called that? No-one mentioned an area of quicksand, it must be a joke.* Finally, the driver slowed down, stopped at a set of gates, and showed his pass to the sentry on duty. The bus took off throwing him forward and backward with a jolt. No sooner had the bus started than it slammed to a stop, with a screech of brakes, outside of the First Aid building. *Great I probably have whiplash now* he rubbed his neck.

The driver helped Trae take the injured soldier inside the First Aid building. Trae couldn't help but notice that all the buildings at the base looked the same – cream brick with iron roofs.

The only distinguishing feature that separated them, from the First Aid building, was the big red 'H' symbol that was painted on the walls. If he wasn't in so much pain, he would've appreciated the symmetry, and the order.

'What happened?' the nurse on duty looked at them, before pressing a buzzer on the desk. A couple of nurses suddenly appeared, and took the injured man away, into a room that was partitioned off, so a doctor could look after him.

'The helicopter crashed' the driver offered before turning to Trae. 'Well, I'll leave you in her capable hands.' Trae watched him leave, as another nurse appeared and showed him to another room, which had been partitioned off, to wait for a doctor.

Trae sat on the stretcher bed and waited for the doctor. He breathed in deeply. Most people hated the smell of disinfectant, but he didn't mind it. At least, it was a sign the place was clean, and neat.

As he waited for the doctor to come, his mind drifted back to his arrival, and he wondered, just what it was that he had walked, or rather flown into? *What on earth was going on in this peaceful, idyllic island?*

'Well, Trae' the doctor finished cleaning up his wounds. 'I reckon you should go and buy a lottery ticket. Apart from a few cuts and abrasions, the only damage you seem to have, is torn ligaments in your foot. The nurse will get some crutches for you, but you can leave.'

'Thanks.' Trae took the crutches that were offered and hobbled out to the waiting area. As he waited for his discharge papers to sign, he noticed a young woman sitting in the waiting area reading a magazine. *Well, who are you, gorgeous?*

She looked at her watch and put the magazine on the chair next to her. She stretched and yawned. As she did so she looked over in Trae's direction. She smiled and stood up. As she did so, she pushed her shoulder length red hair up under her cap. 'Colonel Watkins' she walked over to him. 'Good to see you made it. I'm Staff Sergeant Perry but you can call me Sloane.' She shook his hand, then took a step back, and looked at him. 'You should change your clothes before I take you to the office.'

'My clothes blew up.' *Oh no, I didn't say that did I. I wanted to appear cool, calm, and collected.*

Sloane smiled, almost as though she knew something that he didn't. 'Ah yes the chopper accident.'

'Are you serious? That was no accident!' Trae spat out. *So much for being cool, calm, and collected* 'What's going on here? What did I fly into, a warzone or something?'

'Or something' Sloane said cryptically. 'Either way, you can't go to the office like that.'

'Aren't I staying here at the base?'

'No. You have been hand-picked by the grenadier. Don't worry, there's a lot of accidents at the office. Trust me, you will be more useful there, than here.' Sloane held the door open for him. 'We'll stop at supplies and get you a new uniform, it's the next building over.'

That's good. Wow, to think that I have been handpicked. Trae cheered up as he hopped alongside Sloane as they went to the next building to get a new uniform. *The respect I've been searching for I'm sure I will find here.*

'That's Rodney' Sloane said as they passed a kangaroo in a pen eating some grass.

Trae stared at the kangaroo, and the pen it was in. 'Is that rolled up sticky tape being used as fencing wire?'

'Huh' Sloane looked at the fence, shrugged, and continued walking to the supply building.

'What are you looking at, bud' the kangaroo said as Trae stared at him.

Whoa, did you just talk to me?

'Something wrong, Trae?' Sloane asked as she noticed he had stopped and was staring at the kangaroo.

'Um, er, no' Trae started to hobble after her to the building. *I must have concussion. I am not going to say Rodney talked to me.*

'Chuck!' Sloane yelled out as she shut the door behind Trae 'Get out here!'

A young soldier ran in from out the back. 'Sorry, Sloane I was stock taking.'

'Trae here needs a new uniform' she said as she looked at her mobile that buzzed.

'I'm a medium' Trae said. His face reddened as Chuck laughed.

'Yeah, right. Trust me, with your stomach, you want a large.'

'I'm not that fat' Trae muttered and handed his crutches to Sloane. 'Do you have a change room?' *I'll prove I'm not a large.*

Chuck looked through the shelves, and handed Trae a pair of trousers, t shirt and shirt. 'That's the change room' he pointed to a curtain that was hung up on a curtain rod.

'Do you need a hand?' Sloane asked.

'I'll manage.' Trae limped up to the curtain, and carefully pulled it to one side, and went behind it. He looked at the mirror on the wall, well at least he had a mirror to make sure he looked presentable.

He put the clothes on the chair that sat near the mirror. *I look a mess* he took his torn shirt off and put the new one on. *That feels better.* He took of his trousers and started to put on the new pair. As he pulled the second leg over his foot, he saw something under the chair. *Oh wow, that's a Polaroid.* He reached under the chair, but as he pulled it out, he forgot that his trousers were still around his ankles, and took a step backwards onto his hurt foot.

'OW!' he stumbled and fell towards the curtain. He grabbed at it to steady himself and fell through it. With a bang, he landed on the floor, in front of Sloane and Chuck, the camera still in his hands.

'Are you okay?' Sloane asked trying not to laugh at Trae in his state of undress 'nice boxers. Do you normally wear white with pink hearts?'

Trae ignored her, and looked at Chuck 'I found this Polaroid, can I have it?'

'Sure, no one uses them anymore. I don't even know how it got there.'

'Cool' Trae stood up and put the strap around his neck 'I can't wait to use it.'

'I take it the large fits you' Chuck said at the same time Sloane told Trae to pull his pants up.

'Yes' Trae admitted as he pulled his trousers up. *Must be a small make.* He took the crutches back from Sloane.

'Let's go' she held the door open for Trae. Trae followed her out to the car that was waiting outside. As he was about to get in, he heard someone yelling, and a group of soldiers were running towards them.

When they were level with the car, the leader screamed at the soldiers 'Drop, and give me a hundred.'

'A hundred' Trae said to Sloane 'but we don't do that anymore.'

'That's Dr Pain our previous medic turned fitness expert.'

'Medic! Pain was a Medic! Hang on, a fitness instructor? In what? ... Torture!'

'Don't worry about Pain. He came with good qualifications. Now get in the car' Sloane held the back door open for him. She shut the door, then went around to the other side, and sat behind the driver. 'Thank you' she shut the back door 'you know where to go.'

Trae looked at the driver, who adjusted his hat before taking off. *Why does he look familiar?* He looked at Sloane 'So, hand-picked by the grenadier, you say.'

'What?' Sloane stopped tapping on her mobile. 'Oh, well technically, he's from one of those Special Forces branches or something. He's a major, and does Human

Resources, but man, does he like to toss things on the battlefield, so we call him the grenadier for short.'

No, no, no. This was a new start – a new beginning, a new chance of getting some respect away from all the tossers I know. Stop. Breathe ... I was hand-picked, that meant I am wanted, I am accepted, I will be respected. It's going to be good, just relax.

He watched the buildings flash by as they entered the town limit. 'So, why am I not at the base?'

Sloane half grinned. 'Well, there are already a few medics at the base, but someone special is needed for headquarters. Don't worry; there will be plenty of accidents, and injuries for you to attend to. You will be kept quite busy.'

Trae stared into the rear vision mirror, at the driver. *Where have I seen him before?* He blinked, to readjust his eyes from the lack of sunlight, as the car slowed down, and entered an underground car park.

'Whoa' Trae said as the driver pulled his cap off 'it's Roger. What's he doing driving the car?'

Sloane looked up from her phone. 'You mean Raymond. We get short staffed. Whoever is capable, jumps in and helps.'

'But he's a kangaroo!"

Bang Rodney drove into one of the pylons.

'You idiot, you can't drive' Trae said.

'You're telling me. I'm a kangaroo. I have short hands, see.' Rodney got out of the car 'Driving is not the job for me.' *Boing, Boing, Boing* he hopped away.

'I can't believe you let him drive.'

'Trae!' Sloane warned as she got out of the car to assess the damage 'do you have a problem with Ralph?'

Trae got out of the car and continued his rant 'I thought it was Rick. He's a kangaroo!'

'There's no discrimination here' Sloane shrugged as she took photos of the damage.

'But he … and then he …'

'Trae, you're starting to jibber jabber. Do you want me to put you on report?'

'No.' Trae took a deep breath 'Maybe I'm just a bit concussed.' *How come she treats a kangaroo like a person. It doesn't make sense.*

'There you go' Sloane pointed to the lift that the car had stopped in front of. 'Take the lift to the top floor and you'll find reception. They're waiting for you. Good luck.'

Good luck, why would I need good luck. Trae walked to the lift. The doors opened the moment he pressed the button. He stepped in and turned around to face the now closing doors. *Guess I'll find out.'*

The lift was silent in its ascent to the top floor. Trae watched the floor numbers light up as the lift passed them. With a sudden stop, the doors opened; he stepped out, and found himself facing the receptionist's desk.

'Colonel Watkins' the receptionist, impeccable groomed stood, and extended her hand. She shook hands with him 'I'm Isabella.'

Trae was surprised at the firmness of the grip she had when she shook his hands. 'You're awfully close to the lifts.'

'Yes, it's for a fast get away' she handed him a clipboard 'please sign in.' After Trae had signed the board; she took it back and handed him a pass. 'This is your temporary pass until we get you a new one organised.'

'Thanks, what do you mean for a fast get away?'

'Oh. Nothing really, you can go through to the commander's office' she pointed to where a group of people were standing. 'It's right at the back, go passed that group of people, and you can't miss it.'

Trae could hear people chanting something, but he couldn't quite make out what it was because of the distance. 'Is something going on? What are they saying?'

'There's always something going on' Isabella smiled and sat down. 'The commander has to deal with something first, but he won't be long.' She waved Trae through as she answered the phone.

The chanting grew louder as Trae walked towards the commander's office. 'Aaronn, Aaronn,' the chant was hypnotic, and Trae found himself being drawn to the crowd.

Trae pushed his way through the crowd to see what was happening. 'Oh my...' Trae surprised at what he saw, stepped backwards, and trod on someone's foot. He was pushed forward again. He looked upwards, and mouthed 'Why?'

A man in army trousers, and a t-shirt was brawling with an octopus, which was wearing a red scarf between its eyes, and tentacles, and a black fedora.

'Aaronn, Aaronn' the crowd chanted.

'C'mon, Aaronn!' one of the people in the crowd yelled 'you can beat him!'

'Yeah, Aaronn' the octopus spoke 'you can beat me.'

Trae's mouth dropped open momentarily when the octopus spoke. He didn't know what was going on, but he certainly didn't expect the octopus speak, and with a somewhat dulcet, high-pitched voice, at that. *This day was getting weirder by the minute.*

'Then stop cheating' the man called Aaronn seemed to be using all his strength to try and control the octopus.

'I'm not cheating.'

'Then, put the private down!' Aaronn ordered.

'Why?' the octopus twirled a screaming man in his tentacles. 'He's my favourite nun chucks.'

'I'm warning you, Octavius!'

Wow not only does the octopus talk, but it has a name. Knowing that no one would believe what he was seeing, Trae raised the Polaroid, that he had found up so he could see through the viewer. People laughed at him for using old technology, but he like the feel of the camera.

No one is going to believe an octopus talks. Trae made sure that all three were in the frame of the camera. He pressed the button just as the octopus threw a screaming private, at Aaronn. As the shutter went off with an audible sound, the flash lit up the area, and the octopus yelled 'Incoming!'

'Everyone duck!' Aaronn dropped to the floor as Octavius started to throw chairs, files, tables, people, and whatever else was in his tentacles reach. 'Brigadier, stand down.'

'But the enemy?'

'Is gone' Aaronn stood up now that Octavius had stopped throwing things around 'you have done well.' Aaronn put the fedora back on the octopus's head. 'And you' Aaronn pointed to Trae 'my office, now!'

'Paperwork, paperwork' the octopus muttered as Trae walked past 'that's all I ever do now.'

'Sit!' Aaronn pointed to one of the chairs in his office, as he put his shirt that was hanging, on the back of the chair on. 'Just what did you think you were doing?'

'Well, I've never seen an octopus in the workplace, let alone one that talks. I mean I've heard of experiments being done ...'

'Enough!' Aaronn swallowed his coffee that was on his desk. 'Yuck, I hate cold coffee. Didn't you read the confidentiality agreement you signed? No photos' Aaronn said shaking his head. 'Besides' he took the photo from Trae 'that belongs to the brigadier. I think. Well, it's mine now.'

'I forgot!'

'You forgot!' Aaronn rolled his eyes and mentally calmed himself down. 'Well, I guess you won't forget again, will you?'

'No, but-'

'No buts. You will not speak outside of this office. and remember this; Octavius is a brigadier, which means he outranks you. One word from you, and I'll bust you lower than a private.'

What can be lower than a private? A cadet, hang on that means I'm outranked by an octopus! Are you serious?

'Well, there's no real harm done.' Aaronn stood up 'Come with me and I'll introduce you to the brigadier and show you around. There are after all a few rules that you have to abide by, other than that, everything is open to interpretation.'

What? Trae followed Aaronn out to Octavius's desk.

'Brigadier, I'd like you to meet our new-'

'Traitor!' Octavius held up one tentacle to the side of his mouth, as though he were whispering a secret to someone.

'No.' Aaronn corrected 'Medic.'

'You were the one in the chopper. What happened there? 'Cause, Aaronn blames me.'

'I'm not sure. I saw something fly into the helicopter, and I went to kick it out, but it flew into the front of the helicopter.'

'Wow, Trae, I can't believe you killed all those people.' Octavius turned to Aaronn 'See, it wasn't my fault, it was his.'

'Me? It's not my fault!' Trae objected.

'Really' Octavius stretched and leaned forward 'you were the one who kicked it into the cockpit.'

'Yes' Aaronn interjected 'but who was batting?'

'That is beside the point.' Octavius sat back in his chair 'It probably would've rolled out if someone, I won't mention any names ... Trae, hadn't kicked it.'

'That is enough, brigadier. I want you to treat Trae with respect.'

Finally! Someone, who knows his job, hang on that's an octopus being ordered to respect me. Trae shrugged his shoulders. *I don't care, as long as it's been ordered to respect me, it's all good.*

'Sure, Aaronn, whatever you say.' Octavius picked up an object off his desk.

'Hey!' Trae exclaimed 'that's one of them awards you get for like movies and stuff.'

Octavius looked at the object he was holding. 'Yeah, it's one of a few I have.'

'What would you get one of them for?'

'A music video I did. I'm a drummer in a rock band.' Octavius looked at Trae. 'Maybe you've heard of us – Marvin's Martians Mantra.'

'But they're awesome.' Trae paused as he realised that one of his favourite rock bands had a talking octopus as the drummer. 'No, no way ... Aaronn?'

'What can I say? With eight tentacles, Octavius is a great drummer.'

It's also a good way to shoot traitors in every direction' Octavius laughed.

'You just chewed me out for ten minutes because I took a photo, and you let him make a music video that goes worldwide. What gives?'

'Well, Trae here's the thing' Aaronn paused momentarily 'let's be honest, no one ever notices the drummer.'

'And I wore a wig' Octavius added.

'Which I personally thought was a bit much' Aaronn side-tracked.

'Why?' Octavius seemed genuinely confused 'rock stars have long hair.'

'It's just that you have no reason to have hair in the first place' Aaronn reasoned.

'Hey, wait a minute' Trae interrupted 'you guys haven't released any new material for a while. What happened? Creative differences?'

'Let's just say that we're looking for a new lead singer, and a guitarist, and a base player. Hey, trumpet nose, heads up!' Octavius hurled the award he was holding across the room. A young lad who had the misfortune of having a disproportionately large nose, to the rest of his face looked up when Octavius yelled.

Thunk the trophy hit the young man on the bridge of his nose. 'Yes, bullseye' Octavius ignored the young man's yell of pain and turned to Aaronn. 'I promise to respect, Trae, just like I respect anyone else.'

'Glad to hear it' Aaronn shook Octavius's outstretched tentacle, as he did his best to ignore that Octavius had crossed two tentacles behind his back, and the scene unfolding before him.

'You call that respect?!' Trae looked incredulous. *I don't believe this.*

'No, I call that a B flat.' Octavius laughed at the man's nasal wailing 'Listen.'

'This is one of the brigadier's better days. You should see him on bad days, he can get ... well, scary.' Aaronn shivered at the thought as he looked at the young man. 'Tell you what. You stop that guy's nose from bleeding, and then we'll continue with the tour.'

About half an hour later, Trae went looking for Aaronn to finish the tour. Isabella pointed towards an office, near to where Aaronn's office was. He could see a group of people standing in and around the doorway. As he walked towards them, he could hear them arguing amongst themselves.

'What's your bet ladies and gentlemen' Sloane could be heard the closer he got 'is it a washing machine, or a – a – I have no idea, what this is?' She turned the machine slightly to the side, where everyone could see a hole, because it was missing part of its back cover. She pulled on a cord, which looked like it was braided plastic, that was attached to the machine with a variety of other wires, and cords. 'I don't even know what this is, I've never seen so many cables, and wires hanging out the back of a machine.'

'Of course, it's a washing machine' one of the men in the crowd said, 'look at the lid on top of, it opens and shuts just like top loader.'

'Huh' a woman said, 'it's clear you don't do your laundry, anyone can see it's a a a whatever it is, it's a machine, look at the lights flashing in a bizarre pattern.'

'It could be anything, but I've never seen such a sequence of lights, and knobs, and that one there that's glowing red, says launch' another man said, 'it's quite strange for that to be on a washing machine.'

'It's obvious it's the start button' the woman said. She turned to Sloane 'Here's my twenty bucks, it's a washing machine.'

As the crowd started arguing amongst themselves Trae asked the person closest to him 'What's going on?'

'Harry, the maintenance guy, found this odd-looking machine in the basement when he went to repair something. He had no idea what it could be, but he thought it might be useful up here, so he brought it up and plugged it in to be used, and everyone has been arguing about what it is since-'

'All right everyone' Aaronn ordered 'all of you back to work.'

When the people went back to their workstations, Trae walked into the room and looked at the machine. 'What do you think, Trae?' Octavius asked as he sat on the machine.

'The general consensus is that it is a washing machine' Sloane said as she looked at her notebook 'although Tina said that she just liked the lights flashing different colours, she thought it was sending some sort of coded message.'

'I agree' Aaronn said, 'it's a washing machine, and you had better get off it, before it breaks, Octavius. Do you want to take it home with you, Sloane?'

'That is not a washing machine' Trae said, 'it's a strategic weapons computer. It's an early model but that's what it is. It even has it written in small letters on the side.'

'No, it's a washing machine' Sloane and Aaronn agreed.

'How do you know what it is?' Octavius asked as he tried took as though he was offended as he got off the machine. 'I thought you were a medic.'

'I just told you' Trae hit his palm against his forehead 'it's written on the side; besides it looks like the one I saw in a museum.'

'I wonder what this button does' Octavius ignored Trae and pressed one of the buttons. The lid on top of the machine began to open and shut, and smoke started to come out.'

'I don't like the look of this' Sloane coughed as she switched the power off and unplugged the cord.'

The machine's top lid began to open and shut, as it breathed fire out and began to laugh. 'I will kill you all. I hate all humans.'

'What about octopuses?' asked Octavius. 'What about me?'

'Octopuses don't go to heaven' the machine laughed. 'Indignity after indignity.'

'I hate all living things. I think you are all disgusting, vile creatures and you shall all die a horrible death of my choosing, when I choose it.' The machine began to crab walk out of the room, and when it could it used the wires inside to help leverage it along. As it dragged and scrapped itself along the floor, it laughed.

'What the?' Trae walked out of the room with Aaronn, Sloane and Octavius following him. They watched the machine drag itself at a fast pace run past Isabella, who stood up in shock, as it somehow opened the exit door, to go down the stairs.

'Aaronn' Isabella turned in their direction 'was that the machine, Harry brought up? What happened?'

'Sloane touched it' Aaronn said as he walked to the lift and pressed the down button 'c'mon, Trae, we might as well finish the tour, then call it a day.'

'But what about the machine' Trae asked still trying to believe that the machine had somehow managed to leave the building.

'Most of Sloane's mishaps shall we call them turn up eventually' Aaronn walked into the lift 'are you coming?'

'It wasn't my fault' Sloane protested as Trae got in the lift with Aaronn, and the doors shut. She looked at Isabella who had gone back to typing her notes. 'It wasn't my fault, I just turned it off, and unplugged it because it was smoking.'

'I know' Isabella glanced at her 'it's not your fault.'

Sloane got in the lift to go home 'It wasn't my fault' she told herself.

*** III ***

'Oh, what is that awful noise' a figure dressed in black said

'It's that guy who's been sleeping on the bench the last few weeks.'

'His snoring is loud enough to wake the dead.'

Two figures crept towards Trae. 'Let's have some fun, Magnus' Tupin whispered.

As the night wore on the two figures gathered leaves and spread them over Trae. 'This guy could sleep through anything' Magnus giggled.

Tupin took Trae's watch off, and changed the time, before putting it back on. 'Let's see how long it takes him to figure out it's the wrong time.'

Trae's snoring still echoed in the night air as they walked out through the park.

Trae yawned and stretched. *Damn, this bench is uncomfortable. It feels like I've been sleeping here for months not weeks.* He looked at his watch. *Oh no, I'm late.* He ran from the park to the office.

Huh! He looked at the empty car parks as he walked through the car park ten minutes later to the lift. *How strange,* he looked at his watch as the lift doors shut. Six a.m. *yet no one else was here, yet. Maybe they were all late. Is that possible? Does it really matter? It will give me time to get started on my work and try and make up for all the mistakes I've made since my arrival. I've had nothing but trouble with Octavius.*

Man, what a morning. He yawned *'I'm going to ask General Melon about a place for me. This is no way to treat a person.* The lift doors opened. *It was so quiet with no one around, especially that crazy octopus.* He looked at the clock on the wall behind Isabella's desk, as he stepped out. *Really, four thirty a.m.*

He wandered around and checked all the clocks in all the offices. Every clock said the same. Four thirty a.m. *Well, no wonder no one was here yet, but how did my watch get so far ahead? Actually,* he put his briefcase down on his desk; *this means that I can use the pool before Octavius takes his morning dip.* He wandered down to the recreation room, to the change room next to the swimming pool.

Trae stifled another yawn and changed. He looked at the clock in the change room. Five a.m. *I've got an hour to use the pool and taste the chlorine.*

Aaronn's words echoed in Trae's head. 'You can use the pool anytime you want, except the hours between six and nine a.m. During that time, the pool is off limits, as the brigadier uses it, and he is not to be disturbed.'

Trae slipped into the water and started to stroke his way to the other end. *I so needed this.* He turned at the wall and headed back *a nice relaxing swim before dealing with the day.* He thought of General Melon's description of Octavius.

'Unique' the general had said. *Well, I have a few other words to describe him: lunatic, crazy, psychotic and the way Octavius looks at me.* A cold shiver ran down his spine. *Totally unnerving,* and he wasn't sure, he couldn't prove it, but he was sure that Octavius was accessing his computer. *That crazy octopus, he was a danger to, well, everyone.*

'Morning, Isabella' Aaronn looked at the clock on the wall and then at his watch.

'Morning' Isabella smiled at his confusion. 'All the clocks are ninety minutes behind. They're being changed now.'

'That's odd. Is Trae in yet?'

'I don't know. I was running late, but I haven't seen him yet' she returned to sorting through her emails.

'That's not like you to be late.' Aaronn frowned 'Is everything okay?'

'I'm sorry Sir, it won't happen again. I had something urgent to attend to, but it was a personal matter.'

'So long as you're okay' Aaronn wasn't totally convinced. It was something in the way she spoke, and looked, but he couldn't quite put his finger on it. Isabella was nodding her head in agreement as she answered the phone that was ringing. She hid it quickly, but he was sure he saw something. He had caught a glimpse of what ... evasiveness? He headed off towards his office as she turned her attention to her emails and phone call. *Why were all the clocks wrong?*

As he passed Trae's office, he saw Trae's briefcase sitting on the table. *How odd. General Melon had said that Trae was an early bird; he was always on time, if not early. Some crazy notion of proving himself reliable to everyone, something to do with respect that he was seeking. Still, it was odd he wasn't in his office. Trae never went anywhere without his briefcase. He had to be here somewhere, and the clocks were all ninety minutes behind. Why?*

Aaronn spun around and looked at Octavius's desk. He wasn't there. *Oh no.* Aaronn just knew that Octavius wouldn't let a single inconsistency, in the schedule slip after the war of ninety-eight.

He went into his office and logged onto the security cameras to see if he could pick up anything unusual. He looked at the camera screens one by one. *Nothing, nothing, nothing, noth- Whoa, what?*

Aaronn zoomed up the screen that showed the swimming pool area and put the audio on. Trae was flailing around in the water. He came up for air 'Help! Crazy octo-' before being pulled down under the water again. *What is that around his waist? Oh.*

Who's that? He stared at a figure that was kneeling on the edge of the pool. 'That's it, Trae, breathe the water in. Feel the pain in your body.'

The realisation hit Aaronn just as Octavius surfaced briefly. Still holding Trae under the water Octavius yelled 'Die you traitor! Will you die already?'

Aaronn hung his head briefly. *It's too early for this. I haven't even had my coffee yet.* 'Octavius!' Aaronn's voice reverberated around the office. He ran out of the office, down to the recreation centre, and into the pool area. 'Octavius, stop!'

Trae surfaced and gulped for air. 'Aaronn, help!'

'Brigadier!' Aaronn ordered 'bring Trae here!' Aaronn watched as Octavius swam to the edge, with Trae, still wrapped in his tentacles. Aaron grabbed Trae's hand and hauled him out of the water. Octavius climbed out and sat on the edge.

'You' Trae gasped for air with every word 'you tried to kill me!'

'I wasn't trying to kill you.' Octavius explained 'I was interrogating you. That's what you do with traitors.'

'I'm not a traitor!'

'You disappoint me, Trae' Pain said, 'drowning would've toughened you up.'

'You're nuts!' Trae gasped.

'Enough' Aaronn interrupted the argument. 'Trae, I think you'd better have the day off.' Aaronn helped Trae to stand up 'In fact, I think we should drive you home.'

'I don't have a home. I've been sleeping in the park these last few weeks.' Trae shivered 'It's scary too, I keep seeing black shadows.'

'You have a unit. Octavius was supposed to t...' Aaronn looked at Octavius.

'What?' Octavius feigned a look of innocence 'Oh, yeah. Hey, Trae, before I forget, I have to tell you, you have a unit?'

'We'll discuss this later' Aaronn spoke to Octavius first, and then to Trae 'C'mon, Octavius can drive.'

'First, will you let Octavius drown me' Pain said, and jumped into the water.

'With pleasure' Octavius slid into the water.'

'Hold it!' Aaronn ordered 'No one is going to drown anyone. Pain, get out of here, Octavius let's go.'

'Hang on. Let me get dressed first.' Octavius went over to a chair and put his fedora and scarf on. 'Okay, I'm ready. No, no I'm not, hang on' he bent down, and picked up a pair of sunglasses. 'I found these. What do you think? Now I can blend in better.'

Trae and Aaronn looked at each other, with a look that said, only drugs or a severe case of stupidity, and denial could fool these people. 'You look great' Aaronn tossed Octavius the car keys 'let's go.'

'Um, can I get changed first?' Trae draped his towel around his shoulders.

'Don't worry about it' Aaronn assured him 'who's going to notice?'

Trae weighed up the risk. *No one's noticed the octopus, somehow. Well, if no one can notice that Octavius is an octopus, chances are, no one will notice if I'm wearing bathers.*

They walked down to the car. Trae listened to Aaronn as he told Trae about the unit he had been given. 'Get in' Aaronn held the back door open for Trae to get in, and then shut it after him.

Octavius settled in the driver's seat and turned the engine on. 'I like these push buttons to start the car.' Octavius revved the engine as Aaronn sat in the front passenger seat. 'They're so much easier than trying to turn a key.'

'Always thinking of you, brigadier.' Aaronn put his sunglasses on 'Everyone ready?'

'No' Trae's voice came out as a squeak.

'Did you hear something?' Octavius laughed as he dropped the clutch and reversed at speed backwards. He slammed the brakes on just before he hit the car that was parked behind him, turned the wheel, engaged first gear and took off out onto the main road.

'Slow down, I feel sick' Trae complained as Octavius swerved from one side of the road to the other.

'Don't be such a girl, Trae. I'm a good driver.'

'Octavius is one of our better drivers.' Aaronn paused momentarily 'Second only to Sloane.'

'Sloane cheats!' Octavius thumped the steering wheel with one of his tentacles.

'Still, the traffic does appear to be getting heavy' Aaronn observed 'you'd better slow down.'

'But Aaronn ...'

'Brigadier ...'

'Okay, okay' Octavius listened to the warning tone in Aaronn's voice and slowed the car down. 'Where did all these cars come from?' Octavius pressed down on the horn. 'C'mon, move it.' The person, in the car in front of them, stuck his middle finger up at them. 'Did you see that?' Octavius stuck his head out of the window, pressed, and held the horn down.

'Get your hand off the horn, jackass!' the man in the car next to them, shouted through the car's open window.

'Did you hear that?' Octavius said to no one in particular 'Indignity after indignity! I said move it! C'mon get out of the way. I'm a war vet!'

'Who cares?' the man in the car next to them yelled.

'What? Oh, if being reduced to a desk job wasn't bad enough.' Octavius shook his tentacle at the man 'You can't talk to me like that!'

Doesn't anyone on this island realise that they are arguing with an octopus. Trae, tried to make himself, as small as possible, so no one could see him.

'Why, I'll show you who cares!' Octavius swung the car to the right, and hit the car next to them, which dented the door. Then he slowed down a little, to put a bit of space between them and the car in front, then accelerated as fast as he could, and rammed the car in front.

'What are you doing?!' screamed Trae.

'Arrgh, the noise!' Octavius swung the car to the left and squeezed through a tiny gap to the verge. He drove over the verge and whizzed down several side streets before coming to an abrupt stop. 'Here you go, Trae.'

'Here's your house key' Aaronn stretched his hand, over towards the back seat and dropped the key into Trae's hand.

'Thanks' Trae got out of the car 'I think.'

'Home safe and sound, just like I promised you' Octavius adjusted his sunglasses.

'Safe and sound, are you serious?!' You are a certifiable lunatic!' Trae's tirade was cut short by the wailing of a siren. *Oh great. Now what?* He watched as a police car pulled up behind them.

The officer got out and walked up to Octavius's window. 'Good day, Sir' the officer greeted Octavius.

'Good day, officer, is something wrong?' Octavius acknowledged the officer by lifting his fedora up and down.

'I noticed that you were driving a bit erratically earlier. Can I see your licence?'

'Of course, officer' Octavius took his fedora off, pulled his licence out, and handed it to the officer. 'I think you'll find that everything is in order. But' Octavius dropped his voice to a whisper 'I'm thinking that maybe one of us isn't dressed like the others, though.'

'Octavius' Aaronn warned.

'Everything seems in order.' The officer handed Octavius back his licence 'Make sure that you drive more carefully.'

'What?!' Trae exploded, as Octavius put his licence back in his fedora. 'He's a lunatic and an octopus!'

'Sir' the officer turned his attention to Trae. 'You seem a little agitated, and out of place.'

'Agitated, of course I'm agitated!' Trae fumed 'You're talking to-'

'Sir' the officer cut him off 'can I see your papers?'

'What? I don't have papers!' He slammed the door and kicked it.

'Can you two vouch for him?' the officer addressed Aaronn and Octavius.

'Yes' Aaronn confirmed.

'Really, Aaronn' Octavius looked as though he were thinking carefully 'I don't know. I can't say that I know who he is.'

'Octavius!' Trae choked slightly 'you know who I am! Tell him that you know me!'

'Sir' the officer interrupted 'you will have to come with me.'

'What? Why?' Trae asked exasperated. *I'm going to kill that stupid octopus. How, dare, he!*

'We will need to see your papers.'

'But I don't have papers!'

'You can't be on the island without papers.' The officer stated. 'Now, turn around, and put your hands together like so' the officer made a display, 'in front of you.' Trae did as the officer said, and cringed when he heard the click of the handcuffs as they locked around his wrists.

'Aaronn, don't just sit there!' Trae implored as Octavius sat there cackling.

'Sorry, Trae, the officer has a job to do. I'll see if your papers have been sent through.'

'What? You people make the law up as you go along, don't you?' Trae tried unsuccessfully to slip his hands through the handcuffs 'and why do these cuffs have pink fur on them?'

'It's best you don't think about that right now' the officer started to lead Trae to the police car.

'Are we free to go, officer?' asked Octavius.

'Yes, but drive carefully, now' the officer opened the back door for Trae to get in.

Trae watched Octavius, and Aaronn drive off, before he sat in the back seat of the police car. *I can't believe I've been arrested.*

'I'm telling you, Aaronn, Trae is a traitor.'

'He's not a traitor, Octavius.'

'He interrupted my swim.'

'I told you, Octavius, all the clocks were turned back ninety minutes.'

'That's my point' Octavius headed onto the main road back into town. 'One clock I could understand, but not all of them. One clock is an accident, two are a coincidence, and three or more clocks are a conspiracy. It's all a conspiracy, I tell you.'

'There's no conspiracy, brigadier, but if it makes you feel better, I'll have Sloane look into it for you.'

'That would be good. I'm telling you, there's something not quite right with Trae.'

'You two had just gotten off on the wrong foot. Why given time, I'm sure you two could be the best of friends.'

'Friends! I don't think so! I don't make friends with traitors. His behaviour is to - oh yeah' Octavius slammed hard on the brakes, and spun the steering wheel, so that the car was facing the direction that they had come from. 'doughnuts' he drove up into the drive thru that he had seen, and stopped at the speaker box 'want one?'

'Sure. Why not? Oh, and grab a coffee.'

'Good idea, Aaronn. I haven't had a coffee today.'

'Can I take your order, Sir' a voice crackled through the speaker box.

'Yes, can we have two, no four' Octavius paused 'no, make it six cinnamon doughnuts, and two black coffees.'

'Is that all, Sir?'

'Yes.'

'That'll be thirty-four dollars, and fifty-five cents. Please drive up to the next window.'

'Thirty-four dollars, fifty-five, that's a rip off!' Octavius fumed 'I'm a war vet, don't I get a Veteran's discount?'

'No' the speaker box crackled.

'Indignity after indignity' Octavius thumped the steering wheel.

'Tell you what' the voice crackled through the speaker box 'I'll give you a discount, because you do this all the time.'

'That's better' Octavius drove forward 'still too expensive, if you ask me.' He stopped at the next window 'Oh, I don't have my wallet on me, Aaronn, would you mind?'

'Why is it, I always end up paying?' Aaronn handed Octavius the money.

'Well, at least I get it cheaper for you.' Octavius paid for the order. As Octavius went to grab the order, Rodney dropped it. 'You idiot! I'll have you fired.'

'What's the problem here' a girl appeared at the window 'I'm the manager.'

'This idiot dropped my order' complained Octavius.

'It's not my fault. My arms are too short,' said Rodney.

'Get out of here' the manager ordered 'you've dropped every order today.'

'This job isn't for me anyway. I'm just a kangaroo.' Rodney threw his hat on the ground 'I'm out of here.' *Boing, Boing, Boing.*

'I'm sorry sir' the girl handed Octavius a bag of doughnuts 'I've added a few extra ones for the inconvenience.'

'I'll let you off this time' Octavius handed Aaronn the doughnuts, and coffee to hold. 'And at least I don't hold everything, and drive now' he put one tentacle on each side of the steering wheel, and one on the accelerator, and sped off.

'And the island thanks you' Aaronn sipped the coffee.

'What are you trying to say?'

'Just keep your eyes on the road for once, Octavius.'

'No' Octavius said still staring at everywhere else, but the road.

Trae was still in a state of shock at being arrested. *I can't believe this.* He looked at the cell he was in, as he waited for Aaronn to turn up with his papers. The cell was so small, just room for the single camp bed, and him, to pace a few steps, back and forth. The prisoner in the next cell called out to him 'Hey, what ya in for?'

'Not having papers.'

'Really, I thought they might have done you for indecent dress. The island does have a dress code, you know.'

Trae just shook his head and ignored him. *This cannot be happening. That stupid octopus – How does Octavius always come out looking like the good guy? It's ridiculous that no one seems to notice that Octavius is-* his thoughts were interrupted by an officer delivering lunch.

'When are you going to let me out of here?' Trae looked at the orange juice, and burger that he had been given. *Yuck* he hated mayonnaise, but he was hungry. *It's not like I can be choosey now that I'm a jailbird! Oh, my parents would be so proud of me.*

'That depends on whether your papers turn up or not' the officer handed the same meal to the other prisoner, in the next cell 'although they are debating on whether to just deport you.'

'Deport me?!' Trae said incredulously. 'And how do they plan on doing that?'

'Well, there's the old barge that sometimes comes over.'

'They blew that up!' Trae told the officer.

'Oh well, there's always the helicopter.'

'That was blown up when I came!'

'You sure do have a lot of things blow up when you're around' the officer said, 'I guess you could always swim.'

'Wait, what if he destroys the water?' the prisoner in the next cell interrupted.

'What? That's stupid; I don't even know where I am!'

'You're on the island, and in hot water, of course.' The officer delivered the last of the meals 'I guess they'll come up with something.'

'You know what.' Trae suddenly realised the benefit of being deported. 'Being deported won't be that bad. It means that I'll get off this island, and away from that crazy octopus.' A surge of excitement went through him, and he yelled out to the officer 'Yes, deport me! I don't care how, just, do, it!' *Yes, I'm home free.*

The officer spoke into a radio that previously crackled to life a moment ago. 'Yes, sir' the officer answered it. He unlocked Trae's cell door 'you're in luck your papers have been delivered.'

'No. What about being deported? I want to be deported.'

'I'm sorry, sir but it looks like you're staying here.' The officer led Trae to the front desk where Aaronn and Sloane were waiting.

'Oh, that's just great. You brought her.'

'Okay' the officer ignored Trae's comment. 'All you have to do is sign this form, and you're free to go' the officer handed Trae a pencil with a rubber end.

Trae looked at the pencil in disgust. 'What? Don't I get a pen?'

'Do you have a pen licence, sir?' the officer said sarcastically. 'Just sign the form.'

Trae bounced the pencil, up and down, on the table so that the rubber end hit the table, first. 'Oh, real mature, Trae' Aaronn said after the third bounce.

With all his anger focused on the pencil, Trae gave it one last bounce. 'Ow' Trae cried out as the pencil hit him in the left eye.

'That's great, Trae' Sloane laughed 'try sitting up straight next time.'

'I parked the car, Aaronn.' Octavius came in and saw Trae holding his hand over his eye 'Oh man; did I just miss Trae hurt himself. I did, didn't I?'

'Yes, Octavius, you missed Trae hurting himself.' Aaronn confirmed 'So, Trae, can you see straight enough to sign?'

'Too much pain to care' Trae held his hand over his eye. 'I need a doctor.'

'I thought you were a medic' Octavius stated.

'Yeah, Trae just patch yourself up' Aaronn added.

'Yes, but now, I'm the patient.' Trae stifled a groan. 'I need a doctor, now!'

'Doctor, did I hear someone say they need a doctor.'

'Pain, what are you doing here?' Aaron asked.

'I'm here to make a report. Someone, drove into me.'

'Are you hurt?' asked the officer.

'That's what I want to report, they didn't hit me hard enough.'

'What!' the officer took a deep breath 'Sit down, let me finish with this lot. Right, Trae, sign here.'

'I want a pen.'

'What are you, royalty?' the officer handed him the pencil again. 'Just sign the form. I don't want you here anymore.'

Trae picked up the pencil with his free hand and made a cross on the signature line. 'There. Happy?' Trae tossed the pencil away from him.

'Te-es-ty' the officer took the paper away from Trae. He drew back suddenly as the pencil, Trae had thrown, had flown, and hit the wall, which sent it ricocheting back, and hit Trae in the right eye.

'Ow!'

'Yes. Lightning does strike twice!' Octavius exclaimed triumphantly. 'Trae hurt himself again.'

'Eew, now you have to take it back, it has eyeball goo on it. Take the pencil with you!' the officer threw the pencil at Trae, which hit him in the left eye again. 'I don't believe this! Get him out of here!'

'Yes, a trifecta' Octavius gloated 'and lightning strikes thrice.'

'Alright, Octavius' Aaronn interjected. 'Stop revelling in Trae's suffering.' Aaronn, Sloane, and Octavius left with Trae. 'First stop, hospital' Aaronn decided 'then home for Trae. He's had quite a day, again.'

'What about me?' Pain stood up 'I demand you charge the person who didn't hurt me.'

'Out, out, OUT!' the office yelled 'all of you – Get out!'

*** IV ***

'Hold the lift!' Trae tried to yell but his voice was strained. He was so tired the following morning that he didn't think he had the energy to run, let alone have the energy to yell. Isabella ignored the patch on Trae's eye, and patiently held the door open, till he stepped in, while Octavius stood at the back of the lift, his fedora slightly tilted forward over his eyes. Trae yawned as the doors closed.

'You seem really tired' Isabella pushed the button for the top floor, and then continued texting a message on her phone.

'So, what are you texting, Isabella?' Octavius leaned over her shoulder 'Hey, is that a map?'

'Sorry, brigadier.' She turned, so that Octavius couldn't see the screen, and pressed the send button before closing the screen down. 'It's personal' she turned to Trae 'so, why are you, so tired today?'

'You know those two, twenty-four-hour pizza bars.' Isabella nodded as her mobile buzzed. She looked at the screen briefly before putting it in her pocket and waited for Trae to continue. 'Well, after the guys dropped me off from the hospital last night, don't ask' Trae cut Isabella off as she went to ask what happened. 'Some joker decided to order pizzas in my name. Every hour, someone was banging on my door saying that I had ordered pizzas, and I kept saying I didn't.'

'Ha ha ha, the classics never fail.'

Trae turned to Octavius 'It was you.'

Octavius laughed.

'Well laugh at this.' Trae pulled out a docket and shoved it in Octavius's tentacle. 'I woke up to find this attached to my front door with a knife. They want five thousand dollars. Twelve hundred dollars for the hundred and twenty pizzas, they made, and the rest is for wasting their time.'

'Give it to Aaronn.' Octavius shoved it back into Trae's hand as the lift doors opened, and he stepped out. 'He normally clears up the things I do.'

'That was very funny, brigadier. What did you do with all the pizzas, Trae?' Isabella sat at her desk.

'Well, I ate some, and I stuffed what I could fit in the freezer. The rest – hang on don't encourage him!' Trae stormed off to Aaronn's office as Isabella and Octavius laughed behind his back.

Without knocking, Trae walked in, and slammed the docket down on the table. 'Octavius said that you'd deal with this!'

Aaronn looked at the docket 'Wow, you ordered a hundred and twenty pizzas.'

'No. That stupid octopus did.'

It was then when Trae heard someone laughing that he realised Aaronn hadn't been alone. Sloane had been there talking to him. 'Octavius is such a funny guy' Sloane sniggered.

'He's an octopus!' Trae's face grew red 'what is wrong with you people?!'

'I suppose. Anyway' Sloane continued 'you're just the person we need to see.'

'Why? Is someone injured?'

'Not yet but give it some time.' Sloane smiled to herself 'Actually, I just wanted to know if you had noticed, any unusual activity, on your computer.'

'Sloane's our tech wiz' Aaronn clarified 'and our mechanic, and engineer support.'

'Some engineer' Trae muttered remembering the barge.

'Focus people' Aaronn motioned Sloane to sit down, as she had stood up ready to punch Trae out. 'So, have you noticed anything?'

'Um, well, not exactly. I mean, I did think that someone was accessing my computer, but I just thought it was Octavius.'

'Why would you think that?'

'Are you serious, Aaronn? He tried to kill me, not once, but twice.'

'The first time was not my fault. You did that all by yourself' Octavius looked at them as they all stared at him. 'What? I'm hungry. I thought I'd see if you wanted anything down the shops.'

'That's thoughtful of you.' Aaronn handed Octavius some money 'Grab some milk for the staff room, they're grumbling that there's hardly any left.'

'Back soon.' Octavius lifted his fedora and pulled out his wallet. He put the money in the wallet, which he then placed back into his fedora, and put his fedora back on his head.

'He's so thoughtful' Sloane shut the door after he had left.

'He's an octopus!' Trae dug his fingernails into his leg to stop himself from screaming. *Why did they keep talking about Octavius as though he were a person?*

Sloane raised one eyebrow then continued. 'So, we've noticed an increase in chatter recently, and we think that someone has been tracking Trae.'

'You don't have anything on your computer about Octavius, do you? Hang on' Aaronn stood up to answer a knock at the door. 'Oh, thanks Isabella, I forgot we ordered coffee.' He took the tray from her hands, spun around, and kicked the door shut behind him.

'Thanks Aaronn.' Sloane took one 'Black for me, I know yours is black, Aaronn so, I guess that the white tea is for you.' She looked at Trae, and smirked as she handed him his drink.

'I can't drink coffee.' Trae took his cup, and sat down 'Anyway, there's nothing much about Octavius on my computer ... just a few incidents.'

'Why?' Aaronn drummed his fingers on the table and stared at Trae. He took a deep breath and said 'You need to look at your confidentiality agreement. Which part of non-disclosure, be it written, oral or transmitted in any format did you not understand?'

'But how is keeping a few notes on my computer breaching the NDA?'

'And what if your computer was stolen, and your notes accessed. Now I'm going to have to write that up, and I hate paperwork. Why did you write anything?' Aaronn watched as Sloane put her coffee down and walked behind his desk.

She leaned across in front of him to access his computer, forcing him to lean to one side. 'Don't mind me, but someone has to do some work' Sloane ignored Aaronn as he glared at her before moving his chair to one side. 'I'm just going to check the security footage for the last week.'

'Because he tried to kill me' Trae scratched his head as he finished answering Aaronn's question. *This is unbelievable.*

The room fell silent as Sloane concentrated on the computer. 'There' she said after about forty minutes. Aaronn and Trae stood behind Sloane as she flicked the footage through, frame by frame. 'Check it out.'

They watched a shadowy figure hugging the dark areas of the room as it slowly made its way to Trae's office. 'Who's that? And what's he doing in my office?'

'Take a closer look, I'm not sure, but I think that he is actually a, she.' Sloane walked out of Aaronn's office, and into Trae's office. Aaronn and Trae followed her.

'What are you doing, Sloane?' Trae pushed passed Aaronn and stood in front of her.

'Out of my way, I'm checking your office, genius!'

'What for?'

'A bug, a shadow, a conspiracy – take your pick, but something is not right.' Sloane pushed him aside and started to look around the room.

'Well, if I were planting a bug' Trae leaned against the door frame with his arms crossed against his chest. He watched her pick up a vase and it shatter in her hands. He groaned inwardly *My favourite vase. C'mon, Trae, focus.* 'I'd place it inside the computer.'

'I thought you were a medic, not a tech person' Sloane sat down at his desk.

'I am, I'm not, hey; it was just a random thought!' *And I'm probably still a better tech person than you'll ever be an engineer, mechanic, or whatever other title you hold.*

Sloane ignored Trae as she undid the back of the computer and removed the cover. There inside was a little black box. Sloane sliced the wires that were attached and lifted it out. She handed it to Aaronn and put the cover back on. 'And that, my friends is a bug.' She took it back from Aaronn 'I will check this out later.'

'Good job, Sloane ... hang on' Aaronn pulled out his mobile that was ringing. 'Hello-'

'Aaronn, help me! You promised! Get down here, and bring guns, bring lots of guns!'

'Octavius seems to be in trouble.' He walked out of the office. 'Come on you two.'

*** V ***

'How does he do this?' Trae said aloud as he looked at the scene before them. *What happened? The supermarket – it was so nice, so new, so orderly, and now.* Trae sighed as he looked at the emergency services as they tried to contain the burning pile in front of them. *What did he do? How?*

'Get out!' Sloane's voice penetrated his thoughts. 'There's a tank headed this way!'

They managed to just get out of the car, as a tank stopped menacingly in front of them. Octavius appeared from nowhere, and holding onto his fedora, he hurried towards the car. He stretched one of his tentacles into the car, then pulled it back out, and turned to Aaronn. 'Where are the guns?'

'We brought our own guns, and figured you'd make something up along the way' Aaronn reasoned.

'I said I wanted guns, and lots of them! Which part of that didn't you understand, Aaronn?'

'This is not the place or time!' Sloane started to run as the tank levelled its cannon towards the car. The others ran behind her, towards the burning complex, as a shell exploded out of the cannon, and into the car.

'My car!' Aaronn's voice sounded as though it was being tortured.

'Is no more, Aaronn.' Octavius grabbed a few hand grenades off Aaronn's shoulder belt and ran after the tank. 'Don't worry, I'll get him.'

Octavius threw the grenade at the tank; it bounced off and landed just in front of it. A cloud of smoke erupted. 'Ooh, look at that, a smoke bomb. Shame on you, Aaronn, that's no fun.' Although the smoke started to disperse, it gave Octavius enough time to run, and leap onto the tank. He opened the lid and looked at the guy who had turned to look at him.

'Aaargh, octopus' the guy screamed.

Octavius reached in, pulled the guy out, and threw him to the ground. Then he climbed into the tank which was still rolling slowly forward. 'Now what does this lever do?' he said to himself as he shifted the tank into reverse. 'Oops, wrong way' he shifted the lever and the tank moved forward again.'

'I can't believe he just ran that guy over.' Trae stared at the tank rolling forward 'Where's he going?'

'My insurance company is not going to like this.' Aaronn ignored Trae, as he looked at the few blackened, mangled pieces of metal that once resembled a car. 'It's the third car this year that's been totalled.'

Sirens could be heard as they blared out, so loud that the noise was deafening as the emergency vehicles rolled up. 'You two follow Octavius. and stop him. I'll see what I can find out here!' Sloane shouted, and then realising that Aaronn outranked her, she added 'besides, he'll listen to you, Aaronn.' *Whew, covered that nicely.*

Stop him. Are you serious! 'And how do you suggest we find him? We don't have a car!' Trae looked at Sloane as though she had lost her mind.

'It's Octavius. Just look for the directionally challenged tank, that's shooting everything in its path, and crushing everything underneath it.' Sloane turned away from Aaronn and Trae and headed towards the burning mess. People were sitting, and standing around dazed, a pile of bodies lay to one side, guarded by an officer.

Everyone was doing their job, Sloane noted. The police were taking witness statements, the ambulances were stabilising people, before ferrying them to the hospital, and the fire engines were busy hosing down the building. Everyone was busy as Sloane approached the bodies.

As Trae and Aaronn started to walk in the direction Octavius was last seen heading in, they passed a group of people being interviewed by the local media.

'Oh, you should've seen the brigadier' a woman enthused 'he was awesome – a one man army.'

What? Trae stopped dead in his tracks.

'Yes' a man agreed 'and those fly kicks he did.'

'So, brave the way he helped us out' said another.

Oh, that's it! Trae grabbed the microphone off the reporter. 'He is not brave! Psycho, yes! A lunatic, yes! But he's not brave, and he can't fly kick, he has no feet, he's an octopus! HE'S AN OCTOPUS!'

The crowd was stunned momentarily. The reporter grabbed the microphone back. 'Were you there, Sir?'

'No, I wasn't there!' Trae paused, and looked at the reporter 'Hey, you're that kangaroo, Richard, you're not a reporter.'

'You're telling me. I'm a kangaroo, I literally have no business doing these jobs' Rodney chewed the flowers on a woman's hat. 'I'm out of here.' *Boing, Boing, Boing*

'How dare you speak about the brigadier like that!' a woman yelled at Trae. She turned to Aaronn. 'This man should be court-martialled for insulting the brigadier like that!'

'Trust me lady, this island is punishment enough.' Aaronn grabbed Trae by the arm and pulled him away from the group. 'Not, another, word!' he said through clenched teeth, as he marched Trae off, to find Octavius.

Sloane showed her ID to the guard, so that she could get access to the deceased. Bodies lay in rows with sheets over them as they waited to be removed and identified. Sloane went to the first body, squatted down, and lifted the sheet. She shook her head and lowered the sheet; the body was burnt beyond recognition.

She went to the next body and lifted the sheet. This one was in better shape albeit was minus his head, but he had on his wrist a tattoo symbol – an upside down kite diamond, with an eye in the middle, and a snake wrapped around it.

'I know that symbol' she said quietly to herself 'it's ECI. The Evil Corporation Incorporated – but they had their operations shut down in ninety-eight. Oh, there were a few skirmishes with wannabe's, small pockets that aligned themselves with the Evil Corporation Incorporated, but the main body, they were shut down. I'm sure of it.'

She checked the other bodies. They were the same; all had the symbol of the Evil Corporation Incorporated, although in the last one she noticed a bulge in his shirt. She checked that the guard was not looking, then put her hand in the person's pocket and pulled out a flash drive out. She held it briefly and then put it in her pocket. *This was not good.* She stood up and winced as her knee cracked as she stretched. She sighed and shook her head. She knew what this meant. Trouble, nothing but trouble.

The emergency teams were working hard to put the fire out and get the injured treated enough to be transported to the hospital, which would be full tonight, she noted in her notebook. Sloane started to walk to the to the main road. They would be removing the bodies soon. She hailed a taxi and sat in the back seat.

She sent messages to the Chief of Police, to remind him to make sure that the reports were on Aaronn's desk, first thing in the morning, as the army would be taking over the investigation. 'Yes, yes, I know' she muttered 'I know you're angry, but you don't have to use that language.' She closed the flap of the mobile and concentrated on what she had seen.

'Hey, Miss' the taxi driver stopped his cab. 'You sure this is where you want to go? It's a vacant block.'

'Yes, thank you' Sloane took some money out, and gave it to him.

'Are you absolutely sure this is the address?'

The tone of his voice irritated her. 'I paid you to drive, not question me!' she slammed the door. The driver stuck his arm out of the window, as the taxi took off, with his index finger pointed towards the sky.

'Same to you' she yelled as she walked around the corner to where the entrance to the underground car park was. *Well, at least I know where Octavius is.* She smiled and half laughed as she looked at the tank now parked half on the footpath, half on the road with a car underneath its track. 'Nice parking, Octavius, I'm impressed' she said to herself.

She made her way to Aaronn's office. 'I see you found him.' Sloane walked in and looked at the three of them.

'Yes, he came back here.' Aaronn sat ready at his computer and looked at what he'd written. 'So, where were we? Oh, that's right; you were going to tell me what happened at the supermarket.'

'This I have to hear' Sloane half sat on the edge of Aaronn's desk and looked at Trae and Octavius.

'Okay, so as I was saying' Octavius took a sip of coffee. 'I was waiting in line to be served, when this guy, comes up behind me, and tells me that I have to go with him – that they wanted me back in the lab. So, I told him "No way." And then he said that I didn't have a choice, and that's when I saw the tank outside, and he pulled a gun out. People started screaming, and it was like the war of ninety-eight, all over ag-'

'What war of ninety-eight?' Trae interrupted Octavius's account. 'The nineties were the most peaceful of all times. Ow!' Trae rubbed his leg where Sloane kicked him.

'The war man – it was horrible – the blood, the gore, it was unforgettable' Octavius seemed to lose track in his memories.

'What war? Ow. Stop kicking me, Sloane!'

'Can I kick him too, Sloane?'

'No, Octavius' Aaron intervened 'let's get back to what happened at the supermarket.'

'But I want to kick Trae too.'

'Fine, kick him.' Aaronn gave Octavius permission. 'Anything for a quiet life, then will you tell me the rest? Although I don't know how you ...'

Octavius smiled, bent the tip of one of his tentacles, and swung it at Trae's leg.

'Ow. What the hay?' Trae rubbed his leg 'Aaronn?!'

'Anyway' Octavius satisfied by the outcome of his kick, continued 'I saw the gun, and the tank out the front, and I knew we were in trouble. So, I grabbed the milk with one tentacle, because I know how grumpy some people get when we run out of milk.

I told everyone to get out, via the back door, and with one of my other tentacles, I knocked the gun out of his hand. I grabbed the counter with two of my tentacles, leapt up and out with my others, knocking him over and out cold. And somehow, it escalated from there – my memory is a little fuzzy. I did remember the milk though.'

Well, all of the deceased had the Evil Corporation Incorporated tattoo on their wrist, and I found a flash drive on one of the deceased.' Sloane pulled the flash drive out of her pocket and held it up 'I'll look at it later.'

'I bet it has maps, logistics, and a list of contacts.' Octavius cast a sideways glance at Trae.

'I'm not a traitor!'

'Hey, I didn't say it, but if the shoe fits, traitor' Octavius confirmed his suspicions.

'Trae is not a traitor' Aaronn interjected.

'Are you sure about that, Aaronn? Think about it; Trae – traitor, medic – why, I bet that he's the head of the Evil Corporation Incorporated. Oh man, it's written in the stars.'

'What?!' Trae couldn't finish what he was thinking. He just stared at Octavius. *He's paranoid. Okay, how was I taught to deal with paranoia? Forget that! How, is this, my fault – again?*

Aaronn leaned back in the chair so that the chair was resting on the back legs only. He put one foot on the edge of the desk to stop, himself from, falling, and stared at the computer, thinking.

Octavius reached out one of his tentacles and yanked on one of the chair legs making Aaronn lose his balance and fall off. 'Not funny, brigadier' Aaronn stood up, sat the chair upright and sat down.

'Oh, I don't know. Sloane thought it was funny.' Octavius looked at Sloane who was trying not to laugh. 'As I was saying, it's the war of ninety-eight all over again.'

'Sloane' Aaronn held up his hand in the stop position, to warn Trae who had opened his mouth, not to speak. 'Why don't you take Octavius for a walk, and I'll explain the war to Trae.'

Trae quelled the laughter that rose up in him, as the image of Sloane putting a leash around Octavius, like a dog, and taking him for a walk, played out in his mind.

'Good idea.' Sloane stood up 'C'mon, brigadier, let's go.'

'Do you think we'll find someone who wants to arm wrestle me? I like to arm wrestle.'

'Sure, I can't see why not.'

'What war of ninety-eight?' Trae couldn't help speaking as soon as Sloane, and Octavius had left the room.

'Okay, the war of ninety-eight.' Aaronn shuddered as a cold shiver ran down his spine 'It's a bit complicated.'

'Any more complicated than explaining Octavius?'

Aaronn thought pensively. 'You're right, Trae, the war of ninety eight will be much easier to explain than Octavius. Okay, so it's a really long story, but I'll give you an outline, so you have an understanding, of how horrendous it was. I didn't want Octavius to overhear this, he gets a bit funny, when he hears talk of the war, that's why we don't talk about it around here.'

'Fine, whatever' Trae rubbed his leg. 'I can't believe he kicked me. How did he do that?'

'Octavius is very resourceful. Let's see, where to start?' Aaronn drummed his fingers on the table briefly. 'Octavius was found by a fisherman in the ocean somewhere. The fisherman should've thrown Octavius back, seeing as he was only a squidling.'

'Larva' Trae corrected.

'Are you sure, you're not a marine biologist?' Aaronn looked at Trae 'You seem to know a lot about octopuses.' Trae shook his head in disbelief, and motioned Aaronn to continue. 'Anyway, there was something about Octavius that showed him to be more than the average squidling caught.

When he was caught, he had his tentacles wrapped around another squidling, yelling 'Die Octabius, die.' When they untangled them, Octabius was dead.'

Or, maybe it was the way Octavius latched onto the fisherman's face, or the way he tried to strangle the crew, it could've been just, that they heard Octavius speak.

Anyway, instead of throwing him back the fisherman decided to make a few dollars, so he sold Octavius to the scientists at the research lab, and Octavius fell into the hands of the Evil Corporation Incorporated, and their experiments.

'Where was this research lab?' Trae stood up and stretched before sitting back down again. 'I don't remember anything about a research lab, but then I can't believe a group would be so open as to call themselves Evil Corporation Incorporated.'

'In hindsight the name should've warned us. The island was a classified secret. The lab was originally on this island.' Aaronn swallowed the dregs of his coffee. 'It was found by mistake. A couple of sailors got lost. They managed to let off a distress beacon, which led to their rescue. They said that it was because their navigational gear failed, but when the navy, that was the closest ship to that area, rescued them, they had a lot of empty whisky bottles on board.

Their boat was beached on the sand, and yet somehow, they managed to hole it, but on what, no one could figure out. As you know, the waters are clear; there are no rocks or anything that could've damaged it, but they needed to be transported back, and it was an interesting trip from what I heard.'

'So, the island was found by accident' Trae echoed 'that's unbelievable.'

'The island isn't chartered, and so isn't on any maps. It doesn't really fall into any countries' territory, so as far as the world is concerned, this island doesn't exist. Our government utilised it, and built a state-of-the-art research facility, which is now where the base is. Anyway, many researchers set up there, and for the most part they did what they were supposed to, but there was one group who took research, to an obscured view, and they began to do weird experiments.'

'And this group, would they be the Evil Corporation Incorporated?' Trae groaned as Aaronn nodded.

'They were doctors, and they said that the research they would be doing would advance medicine, but secrecy was very much a part of their research. Rumours grew of what they were doing, and concern was raised with the authorities which resulted in them being investigated.'

'Well, that's a good thing, right?' Trae queried.

'Yes, in theory' Aaronn sighed 'in reality, a whole different ball game. The Evil Corporation Incorporated got wind of the investigation team coming and cleaned up their act. Well, at least they tried to. They locked the door to the lab they were using and started operating from the newer lab next to it.'

'What about the other researchers?' Trae's eyebrows furrowed as he thought about it.' Surely, they would have spoken to the investigators.'

'Yes, but they had left the island. They had a rotating shift. One lot of workers would leave as another team would arrive. Only the Evil Corporation Incorporated, insisted on staying permanently.'

'So, if one lot leave as one lot arrived, what happened?'

'Bad weather delayed the next lot of researchers, and then they had to wait for the investigators.'

'So, they missed each other.'

'You got it, Trae. When they arrived, the investigators were shown around, but when they asked about the locked door, they were told it was a storage room, but that the key had been lost.'

'And they believed them?!' Trae said incredulously.

'Well, there wasn't anyone to say otherwise. At least they thought that, but something strange happened one night. One of the investigators had what he said in his notes was a dream. He heard a voice saying, 'You can find the key in your fridge underneath the caviar, cannibal.'

Trae laughed 'That sounds like something Octavius would say.'

'Anyway, the investigator gets up, and in every room, there was a bar fridge. So, he looks in the fridge in his room, and sure enough, there was a pot of caviar in there, and underneath was a key.'

'Let me guess.' Trae paused as though he were thinking 'It was the key to the locked room.'

'Yes. The investigator was smart enough to check it out while everyone was asleep. When he opened the door, he found the lab with the computers working. He thought they were analysing results, but what he found disturbed him. Apart from the files, he found Octavius in a tank, lying on a piece of foam, sunbaking under the office lights. He downloaded the information, re-locked the door, and went back to his room. He sent what he had back to his superior on the mainland.'

'This is better than a suspense novel' Trae leaned forward 'then what?'

'The next day they confronted the Evil Corporation Incorporated, and all of the investigators were killed. The last thing the investigator had written in his email to his supervisor was that if no one heard, from them the following morning; then they would know that something had gone wrong. No one heard so the intelligence section, and the army, was called in to see what was going on.

General Melon led the team to the island where they found all the researchers had been killed as well. There were bodies everywhere. The Evil Corporation Incorporated had barricaded, themselves, inside the research facility, and they were pretty heavily armed.'

'So, I guess you fought them.'

'Well, I didn't fight them, Trae. I joined after they returned and went on a few peace keeping missions. According to General Melon, the Evil Corporation

Incorporated started lobbing grenades at them, and shooting from machine guns. The soldiers returned fire, but then they heard firing from inside the centre, and people screaming. Taking advantage, they broke through the barricaded doors, found the Evil Corporation Incorporated dead, and Octavius on the floor in the middle of the chaos. And that's how General Melon met Octavius.'

'So, if all the Evil Corporation Incorporated died' Trae began.

'I said we found them dead, but after a head count, they found several were missing. They searched the island but couldn't find them, so they left. Octavius was still quite little, but he attached himself to General Melon's face, and wouldn't let go, so they brought him back to the mainland, and he became our mascot.'

'Now I'm confused' Trae admitted. 'If everyone came back to the mainland, how come this island is a base?'

'Octavius was cute when he was little, but he grew up, and as he grew, so did his blood lust – I mean his antics. He would be in the mess tent and play flying saucers with the plates that people were eating off. Then there was the helicopter incident. Someone brought him on board, and while we were mid-flight, Octavius decided to take over the controls.

He started pressing all the buttons, man, we were lucky to survive that day. He was banned from flying with us, but that didn't stop him sneaking on board, and I'm glad he did. One day we were dropping of supplies, and while we were on the ground the enemy surprised us. Octavius leapt out of the chopper, guns blazing, and dropped all the enemy soldiers. They didn't stand a chance.'

'I'm starting to get the picture. I would like to know how he got his fedora and scarf.'

Aaronn laughed 'He demanded an outfit. Said if he was going to fight, then he wanted a uniform.'

'But' Trae interrupted 'they don't make clothes for octopuses.

'We told him that, but he went down to the supply hut, and demanded one. The soldier just looked at him, and said, 'We don't have anything that will fit you' and Octavius, well he got upset and hopped the counter. He went through everything tossing clothes around until finally he found the lost property box. They were in there, he liked them, so he took them, and he's worn them ever since. But he was getting hard to handle, it wasn't easy to cover up his trail of destruction, so General Melon decided to send him back to the island.'

'So, if Octavius went back to the island, how did it become colonised?'

'The darnedest thing happened. Some of our soldiers started to go missing. One minute someone was there, and the next gone. No trace. The first one was listed as AWOL, but after four, we didn't know what to think, until we got a call from the navy, saying that they had rescued one of our soldiers that they found floating in the ocean. We picked her up off the navy ship, and she said that Octavius had kidnapped her.'

'Octavius kidnapped her, yeah right.'

'Seriously, Trae, we checked the island, and found the missing soldiers there. It seems that Octavius decided that he wanted his buddies back. So, General Melon, thought that it would be a good idea, to turn the island into a base, and a call was sent out for volunteers, to leave life as they knew, and go to a place to rebuild.'

Trae laughed 'How many volunteers did you get?'

'I guess people didn't like their lives. We got more than enough volunteers to go over, but that is another story. And that is the war of ninety-eight.

'That is unbelievable Aar-'

'Hold on' Aaronn answered his phone.

'It's not my fault. I'll try to do what I can!' Sloane yelled down the line.

'Sloane, what's happ-?'

'Watch the news!' Sloane interrupted, and then ended the call.

'Something's wrong!' Aaronn turned on the television screen.

'I always wondered why you had a television in your office.'

'It's for moments like these.' Aaronn pressed the remote, and the television spluttered into life.

'Hey, hey, hey it's the Demon Washing machine hour – and I want to remind you all, that I'm going to kill you. Humans are disgusting. They cannot comprehend the cosmic emptiness of the void that festers in the frail souls that awaits them when their feeble bodies expire. Their rotting carcasses-in-waiting need to be purged! Now back to you, human.'

'Ha ha. Oh my. Those are some very polarising opinions, Demon Washing Machine. Time to check in with the news section of the show but before we can, first a word from our networks sponsor.

The Demon Washing Machine opened its top load lid and spewed out fire. 'WHICH IS ALSO ME! The fires await all! Your only salvation is to be evil and selfish. I bring destruction and ruin to all who –'

'That is not a washing machine, it's a strategic weapons computer' Trae said as they looked at the station which had so much commotion happening between the cast and the crew, that it went off air. 'Wow' Trae watched as Aaronn picked up the remote to turn the channel 'Can you turn it up a bit more as well?'

'I can't believe that thing has a television show. Come to think of it, how is that thing even alive?'

'You were there, Trae, remember. Sloane touched it, but how do you know what it is?'

'It doesn't take a genius to see that it isn't a washing machine' Trae said as Aaronn switched the television to another station and turned the volume up.

'We'll discuss this later, now what has Octavius got himself into now?' Aaronn turned the volume up.

They watched the scenes of angry protesters waving their placards, and demanding that the wildlife in, and near the park be saved, by the park not being included in the island's building projects. And there was Octavius standing in front of them.

'Hey!' one of the protesters yelled 'I've just heard this guy's an octopus! He's not one of us!'

'Octopuses don't go to heaven!' another screamed.

'So much for saving the wildlife' Trae muttered under his breath.

'Shut up, Trae. I'm trying to listen.'

I can't believe these idiots aren't focused on the fact that he's a talking octopus. Well at least they realise he's a murderer.

'Aarrgh!' Octavius screamed.

'Yeah, especially ones that kill!' another protester added.

'It's not my fault!' Octavius began 'they made me do it! Aaronn, help, you promised this wouldn't happen!'

One of the protesters forcefully banged Octavius on the head with his placard. 'We hate octopuses!' Octavius grabbed the placard, and swung it at the protester, knocking him out.

'Oh, this is not what we need.' Aaronn wanted to turn the television off, but instead kept watching. Something flew into the crowd, and an explosion of smoke engulfed the protesters. As it cleared, Octavius wasn't there. 'That has got to be Sloane's handiwork, he switched the television off.

'What now?' Trae stood up 'should we go down there?'

'No. Sloane's driving, they should be here any min-' Aaronn's sentence was cut short by the office staff cheering, and yelling. Some of them were banging their hands on the table, making as much noise as possible.

'Hi, guys' Octavius walked in with Sloane following 'what a day?'

'Octavius, you are supposed to keep a low profile remember' Aaronn sighed.

'You were on television.' Trae grabbed a pad off the table 'Can I have your autograph, Octavius?'

'Oh, did they get my good side?' Octavius looked, in the mirror that hung on the wall, and checked, to make sure his fedora was on straight.'

'You can be such a jerk, Trae.' Sloane took the pad off him and put it back on the table. 'Someone stirred the crowd up. I'll leave you three, so I can finish analysing this flash drive, and try, and stay out of trouble.'

*** VI ***

What, the Trae jerked himself awake, and sat up suddenly. *What woke me?* he yawned and looked at the clock next to his bed. *Two thirty.* He sat up and put his hand on his heart. *I need my sleep, not this stress,* he felt his heart racing as he waited, waiting for something, but what? Sighing, he heard nothing more and lay back down.

After Sloane had left yesterday, Aaronn called it a day, and told them to go home and get some sleep, but Trae couldn't relax, he couldn't sleep. He didn't know why; all he knew was that he was restless. The last time he checked his clock it was twelve thirty a.m. *Two hours sleep, I need at least eight hours, but what woke me?* He yawned, snuggled under the quilt and closed his eyes. *Must get some sleep.*

'And good morning, everyone, this is Zane Hewson with the six o'clock news.' Trae groaned and looked at the clock. *Six a.m. already.* He was so tired that he struggled to sit up. He yawned as the news reader continued 'Breaking news this morning. A passenger plane has disappeared with one hundred and forty-six people on board.

Authorities can only confirm that the plane disappeared off radar. The last thing that the pilot reported was that the compass wasn't working, so the pilot wasn't sure of where they were. Authorities lost contact shortly after. As soon as further details come to hand, we -'

Trae turned off the radio. *How sad?* He hated people being hurt, that was one of the reasons he became a medic. Plus, the army was the only one to provide the security he wanted so he joined as a medic.

But, an entire plane, disappearing – how? He'd better move himself and get to the office. Hopefully, today will be nice and uneventful. Stupid octopus, Octavius was driving him crazy. He was an eight-legged disaster zone. And why hadn't General Melon answered him yet? Surely, he had put forward a strong enough case to get transferred.

'Well, I am not happy about this!' Trae heard Aaronn say as he walked into Aaronn's office.

'What now?' Trae couldn't help, but guess that Octavius had done something, yet again.

'Well, it's about time you showed up' Aaronn looked at Trae. 'Didn't you hear the explosion? Octavius wasn't exactly subtle.'

'I'm sorry, I didn't know.' Trae defended himself 'what explosion?'

'The plane crash' Aaronn turned his attention back to Octavius 'with all the communication equipment at your disposal, Octavius, why didn't you contact them?' Aaronn paused long enough for Octavius to answer but he didn't. 'You could at least, have pinged them.'

'What?' Octavius argued back 'And give away our location. I don't think so.'

'Trae, you need to go look after the survivors. I don't know how, but they did survive.'

'Unlike your crew, Trae' Octavius callously added.

Trae glowered at Octavius. Aaronn pointedly ignored Octavius' comment and continued. 'There are injuries.'

The realisation of what had occurred suddenly dawned on Trae. 'You mean that plane that disappeared was here, and it was Octavius that brought them down.' He smiled, and half laughed. *At least this time it's not my fault.* 'Sure, I'll go to the hospital.'

'The hanger.'

'What? Why are they at the hanger, shouldn't they be at the hospital?' the confusion was evident on Trae's face.

'Only if they need to be!' Aaronn barked.

'And if they start to ask questions?'

'I'll deal with that. Right now, Trae, I need you to take care of them, and keep an ear open. See if they saw anything.'

Trae left Aaronn speaking to Octavius, to go to the hanger, which was really just a huge shed with three sides just outside of the town, on the way to the base. It had never been finished off, nor did it have a specific purpose, but it sounded much better to call it a hanger, than a huge shed that was used for nothing. *How did Aaronn keep so calm? There was no doubt he was angry, but to keep in control the way he did, how did he do it? Was there no law on this island? I am definitely talking to General Melon tonight.* 'Hi, Sloane' Trae walked past Sloane who was coming in as he was going out. 'Did you find anything?'

'Yes, but I'll let Aaronn fill you in. You have enough work to do at the moment.'

'You know?' a look of surprise crossed Trae's face.

'Are you kidding? The whole island knows' she looked at Trae 'except for you, you don't seem to know.' She continued walking to Aaronn's office.

Sloane leaned against the door frame of Aaronn's office and waited, until Aaronn took a breath. Octavius sat, tentacles crossed, and his eyes glazed over, as though he had tuned out Aaronn's voice.

'I have news' she walked in and sat next to Octavius. She patted him on his shoulder and whispered, 'I've got your back.'

'Good.' Octavius pointed at Aaronn ''Cause he's carrying on like I killed someone.'

'Which, you could've done if your aim was straighter.' Aaronn picked up his coffee and swallowed some. 'Yuck, it's cold. Why can't I have a hot coffee in this place' he put the mug on the table.

'Yeah, I was a bit off. I think I strained my tentacle when I kicked Trae.'

Sloane couldn't help but smile as she remembered Octavius kicking Trae. 'Anyway, the crew is working on getting rid of the wreckage, and I know who's after Octavius.'

'I told you, Aaronn – enemies everywhere.' Octavius stood up, and tilted his fedora to one side 'Who are they? And where are they? I demand you tell me! I will fight them-'

'Brigadier' Aaronn interrupted his tirade. 'I think you had better keep out of sight for a while until we have a plan. Why don't you go help the cook prepare for tonight's dinner?'

'But, what about the enemy?'

'They are obviously not going anywhere. We'll make sure that you take care of them. Now go.' Aaronn shut the door after Octavius left.

'Now, Sloane, what have you got?'

'Well, the culprit-' Sloane stopped talking as the phone started ringing. She motioned him to answer it.

'Trae, what's the problem?' Aaronn rolled his eyes and groaned softly 'Uh huh ... uh huh ... you don't say ... okay, I'll be there shortly.'

'Problem?'

'Yes' he stood up 'this will have to wait. I have to go confiscate everyone's mobiles. Someone managed to film a bright yellow light heading towards the plane before it went down.'

'So, what's going to happen to the survivors' Sloane followed him out of the room.

'You know the rule, Sloane. Once you're on the island, you're always on the island. They will have to just get used to their new lives here.'

Sloane laughed as they waited for the lift 'Maybe, Octavius will find someone besides Trae to make his new friend.'

'I doubt it. He's having way too much fun torturing – I mean welcoming Trae to the island' he tossed his mobile that was ringing out of the lifts just before the doors shut 'I'm sick of that thing. I'll pick it up later.'

*** VII ***

'Hi, Tony' Octavius walked into the kitchen 'what ya cooking?'

'Calamari rings.'

'Aarrgh!'

'Just kidding' Tony turned the flame up higher, and started to toss, what was in the pan.

'Oh' Octavius slapped Tony across the back, forcing his head almost into the pan that he was holding. 'You're a great kidder. Anyway, Aaronn says that I should help you. That way I'll stay out of trouble.'

'Yeah, I can always use help. Can you set the tables? The stuffs over there' Tony waved his hand in the general direction of the fridges that lined one side of the room, and a trolley that stood nearby.

Octavius walked over to where Tony pointed at a trolley full of crockery and cutlery. He wheeled it out into the dining room and began to set the tables. A short time later he wheeled the trolley back into the kitchen.

'What?' Tony looked at Octavius as he put the now empty trolley back in its place. 'Finished already?'

'It's quick when you have eight tentacles to work with, Tony, now what?'

'Well, the potatoes need peeling' Tony adjusted the temperature of the oven. 'That should keep you busy, for a while.'

Octavius walked over to the far section of the kitchen to the benches, where a square metal container, that held the potatoes, sat. He started to peel them. One by one he peeled them, and put them into a pot of water, to keep them fresh, till they were cooked.

After one hundred and forty-nine he took a break, and stretched up, his tentacle accidentally, knocking a book off the shelf, that was above where he was working. Octavius picked it up and read the title 'The Health Benefits of Calamari.'

'Really, well, we'll see about that!' Octavius marched over to where Tony was cooking. 'What's this filth?' he held the book up in front of Tony's face.

'Hey, I was looking for that. Thanks, I've spent years working on that book. It just needs a finishing touch. Octavius ... Stop ... What are you do-'

'So, why are we checking out dinner before tonight?' Trae asked as they walked the short distance from the office to the mess hall, which for some reason sat next to the pizza place.

'Because I like to eat in peace, besides the chef always appreciates my input.' Aaronn laughed as his stomach rumbled.

'Oh, and here I was thinking that you were checking up on Octavius.'

'That too, although he really can't get into too much trouble.'

Trae laughed 'Octavius, not cause trouble – yeah right!'

'You need to give him a chance. He grows on you' Aaronn held open the door so Trae could walk in first.

Trae looked at the rows of long tables, each in alignment, the chairs neatly placed, so they were sitting against the edge. The cutlery perfectly placed in order. 'Wow, this looks so different when it's empty.' *So nice and orderly.* 'I wonder what the chef has been cooking.'

'Well, that's what we're for: to make sure that everything is ready for tonight and to feed our stomachs.' Aaronn and Trae sat down at one of the tables, closest to the kitchen door 'Hey chef!' Aaronn called out. 'We're here to taste your speciality dish!'

Octavius walked out with two bowls of what looked like tomato soup with croutons and placed a bowl in front of each of them. 'Where's the chef, Octavius?' Aaronn lifted a spoonful of soup up 'he's normally a bit rowdier.'

'Well, Aaronn, let's just say that he lost his head, and is cooling off.'

'This smells great!' Trae swallowed a spoonful. 'What's this called?' He raised another spoonful into his mouth.

'I call it chef digits.' Octavius jumped out of the way, as both Trae and Aaronn, spat out the mouthful they each had. 'What? You don't like?'

Aaronn stood up, and walked into the kitchen, and looked at blood splattered all over the place. A pan was simmering on the stove, limbs stuffed into pots, the smell from the oven cooking filled the room. Trae followed him in and stopped dead in his tracks as his eyes took in the scene of carnage and horror.

'Where's the chef?!' Aaronn demanded. 'Oh no, what's that in the oven?'

'He should be ready in a minute.' Octavius walked in behind them 'Don't open the oven.'

'Octavius ...' Aaronn paused momentarily, not really wanting the answer, but he knew the question had to be asked. 'Tell me, you didn't kill the chef.'

'Okay, Aaronn – I didn't kill the chef, but where do you think the fingers came from?'

'You killed him!' Trae panicked 'I can't believe you killed him! Why? Never mind about why. What do we do?! What do we do?!'

Octavius picked up the book and shoved it in Trae's hands 'Look at this filth!'

'You killed him because he wrote a book?!' Trae stared at Octavius. 'What, is wrong with you?!'

'Me?!' Octavius took off the apron he was wearing, scrunched it up, and threw it on the floor. 'There's nothing wrong with me, but there is everything wrong with that book!'

'Okay.' Aaronn decided. 'For starters, dinner is cancelled tonight.' Fighting indigestion and rising nausea, Aaronn continued 'and secondly, I am not happy about this.'

'But all my hard work' Octavius pleaded 'I've been slaving over a hot stove all day. Do you know how much blood, sweat and tears went into that soup?! Not mine, obviously.'

Everybody gagged.

'Enough!' Aaron ordered.

'And we will help you clean up.' Aaronn sternly said to Octavius, removing the chef's hat that he was wearing, on top of his fedora 'Won't we, Trae?'

'But, but, what, about the murder?' Trae grabbed Aaronn by the arm. 'This isn't right. It's wrong, it's so very, very wrong.' Trae began to control his emotions – for once. It was too late to undo what had already been done; and they had partially eaten the chef.

'Well, Trae, here's the thing you should know. Technically this island still doesn't come under any jurisdiction. In fact, it's probably best, if you don't mention this to the locals. Could you imagine, if they found out that they could kill and eat each other and get away with it.'

'There's no law. I knew it; you make the law up as you go along.' Trae put his hand on his stomach as a surge of nausea rose up. *This can't be happening. This can't be true.*

'There's island law. We still need to protect people from each other, so of course, we have a police presence. Now' Aaronn handed Trae a mop and bucket. 'Here's a mop and bucket. And if you're going to throw up, do it in the bucket, there's enough mess in here without you adding to it.'

Hours later, Trae went home not sure what to think. He checked his emails before sending yet another incident report to General Melon. He clicked through the email headings. Spam, spam, spam, malware, spam, spam, *hang on. Finally, General Melon's written back.*

Request for transfer denied. *Denied, what do you mean denied? No, I can't be stuck on this island any longer.* Trae dialled General Melon's number. 'What do you mean my request has been denied' he said before General Melon could speak.

'Aah, Trae, nice to hear from you.'

'I WANT OUT!'

'Sorry, Trae, you agreed that this was your last transfer.'

'But, but the octopus is scarier than the motorcycle guy.'

'Yes, yes' General Melon spoke calmly 'I know, but you will just have to find a way, to get along with him. Speaking of Peter-'

'But Sir, he tried to kill me, and he flipped off a passing motorist.'

'Oh, good, it's nice to see that Octavius has calmed down. Why, I remember when ... never mind, we don't talk about that anymore.'

But he also' Trae stopped as a thought dropped into his head. 'General, have you read any of the incident reports, I've sent you?'

'Nope, they're in my "to do" box. Now have a good night. What? Sorry, I can't hear you.'

I don't believe it. He hung up on me. Trae lay down on his bed, but sleep evaded him. All he saw were images of blood. He couldn't un-see the horror in the kitchen; they were seared in his mind, forever.

*** VIII ***

Trae walked into the office the following morning, his mind still reeling from the day before. Everything seemed to be normal. *What is wrong with these people. They were acting, as though nothing out of the ordinary had occurred. But was there such a thing as normal on this island?* He knocked on Aaronn's door. Octavius and Aaronn were deep in conversation. *Didn't these guys ever sleep? They always seemed to be awake and doing something.*

'Hi, guys' Sloane spoke behind Trae, making him jump. 'So, does anyone know what happened to Tony? I had to make my own breakfast this morning and the toaster ran away. By the way, if you want toast, I last saw it heading towards Quicksand Valley.'

'I don't want to talk about it.' Trae choked on every word he spoke.

'It's because you're a cannibal, Trae. Yuck!' Octavius pretended to vomit.

'No need to say anymore.' Sloane sat on the corner of the desk to see if she could read them. They all had the same nauseated and disgusted expression as Trae. I'll organise a letter to his family.' She wrote a note in her notebook, then flipped a couple of pages over 'So, it appears that the Evil Corporation Incorporated have infiltrated the island.'

'How?!' Aaronn thumped the desk 'we have top security.'

'I bet it's that traitor, Trae!' Octavius accused 'Look at him, he's brimming with guilt.'

Octavius, he's brimming with disgust.' Aaronn stared at Octavius with a look that could kill 'And so am I, for that matter.'

'What? I thought we fell under tribal law.' Octavius paused for a few moments 'Which, would explain the cannibalism, from both of you.'

Aaronn clenched his teeth 'Continue, Sloane.'

'It appears, there were a few survivors, who original got off the island by sub. That's how they disappeared, and they've been regrouping, and recruiting, ever since. They disguised themselves, and came over as individuals, and teamed up again when they got here.'

'So, how many do we have?' Aaronn looked at Sloane.

'Not that many, about two hundred, give or take a few. But guess who their leader is?'

Silence enveloped the room as they looked at each other. Finally, Octavius whispered 'It's Trae, isn't it?'

'Maybe it's the chieftain, Octavius' Trae countered. 'Maybe, he has raised the spirit of the chef, you murdered!'

'Octavius, Trae, you're both wrong.' Sloane took a deep breath 'it's Isabella.'

'My receptionist' Aaronn sat back in his chair, laughing. 'You have got to be kidding. There's no way she's a mole; she couldn't hurt a fly.'

'Really, why do you think that she's so secretive?' Sloane asked. 'What, do you think that she's been up to all these months?'

'Uh, filing reports, answering the phone, sitting at her desk near the escape ...' The realisation that Isabella had been acting strange hit Aaronn. She hadn't talked to him all morning. In fact, she had been acting strangely all week – cutting short phone calls, and not letting him see what she was working on. 'Aw, and I thought that she was just suffering, from a random form of insanity that came with the island.'

'She has to die.' Octavius stared at Aaronn 'You know she does.'

'Octavius, you can't just kill people!' Trae couldn't keep quiet any longer.

'Well, maybe you can't, Trae, but ...'

'Tribal law' Aaronn added, as he tossed a grenade, up and down, that he had taken out of his drawer.

'Give it to me' Octavius grabbed it as it came back down.

'No.' Aaronn said 'it's mine' as he wrestled Octavius for it. 'Oh no!' the grenade went flying in Trae's direction.

He instinctively punched at it 'Ow my hand' he watched it roll towards the window.

'Hey, Trae' Octavius interrupted Trae's thoughts of his hurt hand.

Trae looked at Octavius holding the pin from the grenade in his tentacle. 'Oh no' he ran to the window, opened it, grabbed the grenade, and threw it out. As soon as he threw it, he realised that there might be someone on the street. He stuck his head outside, looked down and saw a group of soldiers doing push ups, with Pain screaming at them. 'Look out!' he screamed as loud as he could 'run! No don't look up, run!'

'Yes, the rush of pain. Stand up and enjoy it, men' said Pain.

Trae watched as the soldiers tried to run, while Pain stood there with his arms outstretched as though he were trying to catch the grenade. He turned away from the window as the grenade exploded. 'That is not my fault' he said to them.

'I wonder about you Trae' Octavius glared at him, before turning to Aaronn. 'As I was going to say, Aaronn, was I want to give you the honours, but Trae decided to steal my thunder. But now, it's your turn, Aaronn, and Trae, stay out of it this time.

'I'll go over to the other building, that's opposite this one, just in case you miss.' Octavius stood up 'So, give me five minutes.'

'Whoa, how did you-' Trae looked surprised as Octavius now held a sniper rifle. 'Where did you get that rifle, Octavius?' *He did that so quickly; where did he hide that?*

'One of my many ways, Trae, now shut up.' Octavius walked around to the drawers of Aaronn's desk, opened one of the bottom drawers, and pulled out a headset. He placed it on his head, under his fedora. He pulled out a helmet, and put that on top of his fedora, and shouldered his gun.

Sloane rolled her eyes as Octavius headed out. Aaronn opened the top drawer of his desk and pulled out three grenades and another headset which he put on.

'Off to war, Octavius?' Isabella's shrill voice could be heard in Aaronn's office.

'Something like, that.'

'Where's your fedora?'

'It's under my helmet, Isabella.'

'You look so cute, Octavius, with your helmet and rifle.'

"You won't look so cute with your brains splattered all over the wall.'

Isabella recoiled 'What?'

'Never mind' Octavius stepped into the lift. As the doors began to close, he sent a salute to Aaronn ... and one to Trae. The latter eerily was reminiscent of an insulting gesture.

Aaronn looked at his watch. 'In five minutes, it goes down.'

'You can't kill her, Aaronn!'

'What did I say already, Trae?' Aaronn adjusted his headset and turned it on. 'Tribal law, besides, we're now engaging with the enemy.'

Aaronn looked at his watch. He pulled the pin on the grenade and tossed it towards Isabella. 'Noooo' Trae screamed, alerting Isabella, who reacted by instinctively swinging around and hitting the grenade, with the clipboard that she was holding, so that it landed away from her, and made a run for the stairs before it exploded.

'Nice one, Trae. What did you think you were doing?'

'Sorry, automatic reaction, Aaronn.' Trae paused momentarily. 'No. I'm not sorry. That was wrong. I'm going to see if I can find her.'

'He's so soft' Sloane stood next to Aaronn as Trae stormed off.

'Aaronn, can you hear me?' Octavius's voice, crackled through the head piece, Aaronn was wearing. 'Aaronn, target has been destroyed. And that traitor is there with her body. I can see him shaking his fist in my direction. Oh, what was that? Sorry, I thought I saw something, but I must have been mistaken.'

'Thanks brigadier. Good job. Rendezvous, in five minutes, out.'

'Roger that. Oh no. Look ou-' Octavius's sentence was cut short, as a loud explosion split the air. Fragments of brick and mortar, pelted down on Aaronn and Sloane, as the side of Aaronn's office, blew in. 'Aaronn, do you copy? Aaronn, Aaronn ... Don't worry I'll be there soon.'

Aaronn could hear Octavius, but the headset that he had been wearing, had somehow come off, and was now buried beneath the rubble. 'Sloane, are you okay?' Aaronn helped her up. As she brushed herself down, another explosion shook the building. 'We need to get out of here! Here!' Aaronn tossed a handgun to her. 'You may need this!'

'You think! C'mon!' she led the way through the rubble of the office to the stairs. Aaronn followed her down the stairs to the underground car park.

'Get behind me.' Aaronn pushed her behind him and opened the door that led to the car park.

'Why? Because I'm a girl.'

'No, because I'm the boss, now shush.'

Trae knelt by the body of Isabella, dead at the hands, of Octavius. 'Stop consorting with the enemy' Octavius's voice startled him.

'You, you did this!'

'Well, she's not on the menu. Now, I have to report to Aaronn. I suppose, you have to report to the Evil Corporation Incorporated, now that Isabella's stepped down.'

'She didn't step down. You shot her!'

'Did I? Details, details, details ... the question, Trae, is, are you with them or us?'

'I said I'm not one of them!'

'Yes, but how can I be sure you're not?' Octavius continued arguing with Trae for a few minutes. 'I know how to shut you up.' Octavius hit Trae across the head, with his tentacle, knocking him out. He opened Trae's medical bag and took out the rolls of bandages and started to tie Trae up with them.

He was tying Trae's wrists when Trae started to stir. 'What are you doing?' Trae groaned. 'Ow, my head.'

'Just, making sure that you can't contact your buddies.' Octavius took out a roll of tape and slapped some across Trae's mouth. 'There that should keep you quiet for a while.' Octavius went off in search of Aaronn and Sloane.

Stupid octopus Trae lay on the floor, and unsuccessfully tried to wriggle his wrists but Octavius had tied the knots so tight, there was no give. He tried to sit up, but Octavius had bound his legs together, in such a way, that all he could do was lie there, or roll himself. He heard a sound. A surge of relief ran through him. He was so sure that it was Aaronn that he rolled himself, out into the middle of the lane.

Oh no, it's not Aaronn it's the Evil Corporation Incorporated he realised as he caught sight of someone dressed in a purple jumpsuit with the Evil Corporation Incorporated symbol emblazoned on it, in white. *Maybe he doesn't see me.*

'Look over there!' a voice shouted.

'There, in the lane by the pylon!' another voice yelled.

Oh, crap they see me.

'The medic!'

Oh, good they recognise I'm the medic – a neutral party.

'Should we shoot the medic?'

What? No, you can't do that! That goes against the rules of engagement.

'Yes. Shoot the medic first. He'll only heal the others!'

'AARONN' Trae screamed so loud that the bandage came off his mouth.

'Oh what? What is that noise? Will someone gag him back up before he alerts someone!' One of the Evil Corporation Incorporated yelled.

'Man, Trae sure can scream' Sloane whispered to Aaronn. They had just come out of the last stairwell, as Trae's scream, echoed through. Crouching they made their way across the car park. Aaronn held up his hand to signal Sloane to stop and pointed. They watched as one of the Evil Corporation Incorporated had his foot in Trae's mouth, and another couple were trying to bandage Trae's mouth up. The look Sloane and Aaronn gave each other said it all. *Are you serious?*

'Move your foot!' One of them yelled.

'No. He'll scream again!'

'Why haven't we shot him yet?'

'I don't want my foot shot!'

'Then, remove it, so we can shoot him!'

Shots rang out in the car park, and the Evil Corporation Incorporated dropped to the ground. Octavius walked over to Trae and squatted down beside him. 'You're good, I'll give you that. I leave you for five minutes, and you still managed to contact your buddies – bound and gagged even; now that's dedication.'

'You okay, Trae?' Sloane reached the two of them before Aaronn 'Did they hurt you?'

'Them?! Octavius tied me up!'

'Octavius?' Aaronn looked at Octavius.

'What? I just got here and shot them. How could I do this?'

Aaronn nodded in agreement. 'True, we did see the Evil Corporation Incorporated trying to gag you, Trae.'

'Well, no one's hurt. Let's go kill the rest of them' Octavius headed off.

'Hey! Untie me!'

'Oh yeah' Sloane went to untie him, and then stopped.

What are you waiting for? Oh no, the humiliation just doesn't stop he realised as Sloane pulled out her mobile. 'Gather, round Trae, everyone. Time for selfies.' They gathered around Trae. Sloane adjusted the camera. *Click* 'Perfect. Hey, let's upload this to the internet.'

'But I thought this island was top secret.' Trae said as a wave of embarrassment flooded him. *I don't want this picture on the net. Once something's posted on there, it stays there, you can't get rid of it.*

'True, and normally I'd agree with you, Trae, but this is a shot that just screams to be shared. Besides' Aaronn took the mobile from Sloane, looked at it, and handed it back 'people will be looking at you, not Octavius. Send me a copy.'

'Sure Aaronn' Sloane hit a few buttons on her phone as they started to walk off 'done.'

'Uh, guys.'

'Oh yeah' Sloane came back and untied him. 'Fancy getting tied up by the Evil Corporation Incorporated.'

'I wasn't! They didn't! It was Octavius!'

'Oh yeah, that's right, blame the guy who's different' Octavius complained.

As they were arguing a man in his thirties ran up to them. 'Please, someone shoot me. I don't want to live anymore. Everyone has gone nuts; I can't take it anymore.'

'And now' Octavius raised his rifle 'you will see, natural selection, at work.'

'Noooo' Trae slapped the back of the rifle, somehow making it kick back and fire. 'Oh no' he rushed to help the man who just got shot 'the bleeding won't stop.'

'Wow, Trae!' Octavius slung the rifle around his neck 'and that was in cold blood. Now, stop taking my kills!'

'I wonder, Trae' Aaronn interjected 'have you ever thought of, maybe, not helping people?'

'Oh, I don't know, Aaronn' Octavius adjusted his helmet 'I think he's off to a good start. There was the chopper full of people when he first came here, then Isabella, and now this guy, yeah, he's off to a good start.'

'I thought you shot Isabella?' Aaronn said.

'Minor detail, Aaronn. Isabella's dead, and now this guy, yeah, Trae's off to a good start' Octavius laughed.

'He's dead!' Trae stood up. 'I, I can't believe he died on me.'

Sloane held her hand up to silence them. As they listened, they heard a slight scuffling sound. Sloane ran in the direction, leapt over a pile of rubble, and pointed her gun at the source of the noise. She dropped her gun to her side as she saw that it was a small boy. 'It's a child!' she called out. Holding her hand out, she waited, until he took hold of it, then she pulled him up, seated him on her waist, with her arm around him, and carried him back to the others.

'Oh look, it's a little fledgling' Octavius shook the child's hand.

'What?' Trae exclaimed 'he's not a bird?'

'Well, he's not a squidling, Trae.'

'Octavius, what's a squidling?' Trae was momentarily confused.

'A baby octopus' Octavius told him.

'No, it's not' Trae patted the child on the head. 'A baby octopus is called a larva.'

'I thought you weren't a marine biologist' Octavius reminded him.

'I'm not.'

'Can I hold your gun, mister?' the child spoke to Octavius.

'Sure.'

'Maybe, another time' Aaronn stood in front of the child, as Octavius extended his tentacle, to give the child his gun 'Like another fifteen years or so.' Aaronn looked at Sloane 'You take him to the base camp.'

'Why? Because I'm a girl?'

'Yeah,' Octavius laughed 'because you're a woman.'

'No,' Aaronn interrupted 'because you can drive fast.'

Sloane ushered the child into a nearby jeep, got in the driver's side, and wound the window down. She reversed out of the car park and engaged the gear to drive forward.

'That's right! Get back to your maternal duties!' Octavius called out and started laughing.

Sloane leaned out of the window as she drove passed, aimed her gun at Octavius, and let of a shot as she drove out onto the main road.

'Aaronn, did you see that?' Octavius bent down to pick up his helmet, and fedora that was knocked off. 'Look, she shot my hat. I wonder why she did that.'

'Congratulations, Octavius, I think, you've broken just about everyone on the team.' Aaronn adjusted the backpack he was wearing. 'C'mon, let's go to the bunker, and figure out, what we're going to do.'

'What about you?' Octavius asked as they headed out of the car park. 'Are you broken?'

'One word, Octavius – grenadeball.'

'I thought that was two words, Aaronn.'

'I'd shut up if I were you, Octavius.'

*** IX ***

'Sloane drives like a mad woman' Trae jogged to keep up with Aaronn and Octavius.

'That's how she normally drives.' Aaronn sent Octavius ahead to scout out the area. 'I'm more concerned with her driving it. It's not her car.'

A small group of people ran past them screaming. 'I guess we're headed in the right direction.'

'Will they be all right?' Trae looked at the people running.

'Should be, once, they get to the base camp. Maybe next time they'll listen when they're told to evacuate.' Aaronn listened intently. Amongst the screams and cries of panicked people, the sound of gunfire echoed in the air. 'I think Octavius has found the enemy.'

Aaronn and Trae sprinted towards where the gunfire came from. 'C'mon, Trae, keep up!' Aaronn yelled. Trae managed a short burst, but then slowed down to a walk. 'I think after this is over' Aaronn slowed down to walk with him 'we need to discuss your fitness or lack of it.'

They rounded the corner, and there about ten metres in front of them, they could see Octavius crouched down behind a broken wall. Every now and then, he would stand up and fire a couple of shots, before crouching behind the wall again.

Trae and Aaronn crept forward until they were next to Octavius. 'What have you got?' whispered Aaronn.

'I reckon there's quite a few, hiding in the shop, over there, Aaronn.' Octavius let off another few rounds. 'I reckon, we can get them, if we lob a few grenades over there.'

'It's a bit far' Aaronn mentally calculated the distance, between them and the shop.

'I'll just sit over here while you two figure it out.' Trae wandered over to a nearby pile of rocks and sat down.

'There's only one way' Octavius stated, 'you toss, and I'll bat.'

'Don't forget to empty your rifle this time' Aaronn reminded Octavius.

Oh well, at least they're practising safety Trae watched as Octavius unloaded his rifle and handed the bullets to Trae. 'Don't lose them, Trae.'

Aaronn pulled several grenades out of his backpack, pulled the pin, and tossed them, one by one, to Octavius, who batted each one with the butt of his rifle, sending them flying towards the shop window which was broken.

'Oops' Octavius's voice, jolted Trae out of his thoughts 'heads up.'

Trae dropped the bullets he was holding, and automatically, caught the object that was flying towards him. 'Aarrgh' he screamed, as he realised it was a grenade, and threw it away from them. It exploded in the distance. *Whew, that was close.* He was about to sit back down when an object fell from the sky and landed next to him. Frozen, he could do nothing but stare at the headless corpse.

'Good one, Trae' Octavius patted Trae on the back. 'I really didn't think you had it in you. I thought the others might have been mistakes, but that was well done. You do keep surprising me. Yep, you sure do keep surprising me.'

A squealing of brakes could be heard in the distance. They ducked down, so that the wall hid them, from view and waited as the noise drew closer. The sound of a car engine roared as it screeched around the corner and drove passed them. It screeched to a stop, and reversed back to where they were hiding.

'I can see your, hat, brigadier!' Sloane called out 'Get in!'

Relieved that it was Sloane, they stood up and walked towards the Jeep. The jeep that once was in pristine condition, now had dents on every panel, the windows were smashed, and the front windscreen had a huge crack through it.

'What happened to the car? Trae got into the back seat.

'What's wrong with it? It's still good' she took off as soon as they were all on board. She continued to head down the road that led out of town, towards the air landing strip. Over the bridge, she took the left fork. 'We're nearly there' she turned into a tunnel, halfway down, she took a left into what looked like a wall, but opened at the last few seconds, allowing them to enter into the bunker.

She slammed the car to a stop, the hubcap of one of the wheels rolled forward, then spun around and around, in circles till it landed. They got out of the car, and as Sloane slammed the door shut, the tyres burst. 'Safe and sound' she declared.

'Can anyone else smell smoke?' Trae sniffed the air.

A ball of smoke could be seen coming from the engine. 'Run' yelled Aaronn as the car erupted into flames.

'That's awesome, Sloane.' Octavius dragged the fire hose from the wall and started to hose the car down. 'Can you teach me how to drive like that, Sloane?'

'Sorry, Octavius, it's natural; like fire.'

The extractor fans did their job and got rid of the smoke. Octavius started up the small forklift that was in the bunker, picked up, and carried the charred remains, of the car out of the bunker and re-parked the forklift. 'Yuk, it still stinks of smoke' Trae wrinkled his nose up in disgust.

'It will go.' Aaronn went over to the whiteboard 'Tell us what you have, Sloane.'

'Okay. So, the Evil Corporation Incorporated are all holed up in the courts building, which our sources say is heavily wired up. They have a couple of guards. Speaking of which, why did you guys keep tossing grenades into the shop? All you did was blow up an empty shop.

'Octavius said that there were several Evil Corporation Incorporated in there.' Aaronn realised as soon as he looked at Octavius that Octavius had lied to him.

'Ha, ha, ha. It was an honest mistake.'

'But there was a member of the Evil Corporation Incorporated, that was killed' Trae stated.

'Yeah, you sure broke your Hippocratic oath, Trae.'

'It was not my fault, Octavius, I just reacted.'

'Just, like you did when you first came here.' Octavius paused 'I'm beginning to think that murder, seems to be in you, doctor, if that is what you are.'

'But-' Trae objected.

'Medic, doctor, traitor, it's all the same with you, isn't it, chameleon?' Octavius cut Trae off.

'What?!'

'He was the scout.' Sloane interrupted the pair of them. 'He had set up a computer, controlled mortar. So, you did nothing, but waste ammo.' Sloane started to draw on the whiteboard, an outlay of the building, where the Evil Corporation Incorporated were holed up, explaining as she went along. She turned around to look at them. *Oh no Octavius had that look.* 'Uh, Aaronn, check out Octavius. He has that look.'

Aaronn looked at Octavius. 'Oh no' he said quietly. Octavius's eyes appeared to be glazed over as though his mind was in another time or place 'This is not good.'

'Hey, Octavius looks like he's not here. Check this out' Trae waved his hand, up and down in a vertical line, in front of Octavius's face 'nothing. Not even a flinch.'

'I wouldn't do that' Aaronn warned.

Too late, *smack* Octavius swung his tentacle, and sent Trae flying backwards. Trae sat up and rubbed his jaw as Octavius walked over to the steel cabinets that lined one of the walls and opened one of the doors.

He pulled out several guns for himself and tossed a revolver to Aaronn and Sloane. Then he walked back to the group, picked up Aaronn's backpack, and went back to the cabinets. He opened another door and started to fill the backpack with grenades and ammo. When it was full, he came back to the group and shoved the backpack, into Trae's hands. 'Carry this. All of you follow me.' Octavius headed out with the others following him.

'Aren't you supposed to be leading, Aaronn?' Trae whispered as he fell in line.

'You want to argue with him. He has eight weapons, besides he's not here. he thinks he's back in the war.'

'So, we follow a lunatic.'

'Yes, Trae' Aaronn confirmed 'we follow a lunatic, for now.'

It was dark as they left the bunker. All was quiet, as they silently walked the roads. Not a sound, bar the hooting, of an owl. Octavius cocked one of his guns, aimed it in the general direction, of the owl hooting, and fired. A small thud followed, as the owl's lifeless body, fell from its perch.

Slowly they made their way, through the city streets to the building, where the Evil Corporation Incorporated were holed up. They positioned themselves, nearby, crouched low, they used the piles of rubble that once, used to be walls of shops to hide, themselves. Octavius looked through a set of binoculars that he unslung from their resting place, around his neck, at the doorway of the courts building.

'He can't possible see anything, it's night' Trae whispered.

'You want to argue with him, go right ahead, but they're night vision goggles.' Aaronn sat on the ground and waited.

'Right' Octavius turned to face them. 'There's two on guard duty. You lot wait here, until I signal you.' He handed the night vision goggles to Aaronn 'You may need these.'

'What's the signal?' Trae yawned involuntarily.

'You won't miss it.' Octavius adjusted his helmet and slunk off across the ground.

'Can you see anything?' Sloane whispered to Aaronn, as he looked through the night vision goggles.

'I'm so glad, he's on our side' Aaronn whispered. 'Shush, Sloane.' Aaronn stared through the goggles at the two guards that were in front of the doorway. One had just lit up a cigarette when they both, in quick succession, dropped silently to the ground, their throats, deftly slit. He watched as Octavius then picked up one of the bodies, and hurled it through the front doorway, triggering the trip wire that had been set up.

'Let's go!' Aaronn yelled.

'But Octavius said to wait for the signal.'

'Traemond, in case you missed it, there are bodies flying about, and a massive explosion. That is signal enough.'

'My name's not Traemond!'

'Stop being passive-aggressive, Traemond.' Sloane slapped him across the head, and ran after Aaronn, towards the building.

Trae caught up with them at the front door. 'I am not passive-aggressive!'

Sloane and Aaronn ignored him and entered the building. The room was littered with bodies, blood splattered all over the place. 'Careful' Aaronn warned 'you never know what will happen next.'

He had barely finished speaking, when the roof above them, came crashing down. They could hear Octavius laughing in the distance. 'Oh, he is having, way too much fun.' Sloane brushed the fragments, from the ceiling, off her clothes.

'C'mon, up the staircase' Aaron led the way. They climbed up four flights of stairs, by-passing, the first floor that was no longer there. The stairs were surprisingly strong, albeit a few were rickety, and most of the walls were gone, off the first floor.

As they walked up the stairs, Sloane wondered how the stairs actually stayed standing. She was sure that a few should have collapsed when she stepped on them, and yet they stayed intact.

'I'll just check the coast is clear' Aaronn opened the door they had come to. Aaronn looked at the big number two that had been painted on the door. *This should be the second floor* he reached for the handle and pushed it down. He pushed it open. 'Duck!' Aaronn ducked down, just as a body flew over his head and into the stairwell, colliding with Trae and sending him falling backwards a couple of stairs. 'You all right, Trae?'

'Nope, he's out cold.' Sloane kicked the body off Trae. 'So, you wanna bet twenty he screams, when he wakes up?'

'Done' they shook hands. They waited for a short time, knowing Octavius had the situation, well under control. It seemed to take ages but was only a few minutes before Trae began to stir. He moaned as he opened his eyes.

He saw the headless body next to his feet. 'Aarrgh!'

'Yes, I win!' Sloane held her hand out to Aaronn 'pay up buddy.'

'That's a, a dead body.'

'Yes, Trae, there's lots of dead bodies.' Aaronn patted him on the shoulder. 'Now, check yourself out. We've got work to do.'

When Trae declared that he was fine, they walked up the next flight of stairs to the third floor. Aaronn opened the door, and they walked into the room, guns drawn. Octavius was surrounded by, eight, Evil Corporation Incorporated. Each had a gun pointed at Octavius, and he had a gun, pointed at each of them.

'Hi, guys you're just in time for the finale.' Octavius pulled the triggers, on the guns simultaneously. The Evil

Corporation Incorporated that had surrounded him dropped to the floor, dead, not one managed to get off a shot in return. 'Yahoo! And that is the last of them!' Octavius let off a couple of random shots to celebrate.

'Ow!' Trae yelled as he dropped to the ground. 'You idiot, you shot me' he held his hand over his foot, as he tried to stem the flow of blood from where he had been shot.

'Oh. Want me to bandage it up for you.' Octavius put his weapons down, walked over to Trae, and pulled out a roll of bandages from Trae's med kit. 'I'm really good at bandaging things up.'

'No!' Trae grabbed the bandage of Octavius and started to bandage his foot up. 'I'll do it myself!'

'I thought you couldn't heal yourself, liar.'

'Get away from me, Octavius' Trae said through clenched teeth 'you are my worst nightmare.'

'Boy, he's a bit testy tonight' Octavius whispered to Aaronn.

'C'mon, Trae' Sloane helped him stand up 'let's get you to hospital.'

'Only, if Aaronn drives.'

'What's wrong with my driving?'

'Or mine?' Octavius added.

'And I keep telling you two, reverse, is not a driving gear, and you can't, substitute the brakes, with the handbrake!' Trae leaned on Sloane's shoulder as they made their way out of the building. 'And there are in fact two lanes, for a reason!'

'But they're all on the same road!' Sloane protested as she shut the door after Trae got in.

*** X ***

'So, Aaronn' Sloane walked into, the temporary building that served as an office, while theirs were being rebuilt, the following morning. 'Have you spoken to Trae, today?'

'No. Why?'

Sloane looked in the mirror that was hanging on the wall and adjusted her hat. 'I hate dress uniforms.' Satisfied she turned to Aaronn and adjusted his tie for him. 'He just didn't seem himself at the hospital, and then, he turned up at my front door, at two a.m. this morning, and asked if I had a dress.'

'How odd, you have a dress?'

'Sure. Remember that fancy dress party, a few years back? You went as a pirate, Octavius went as a dog, and I went as a woman.'

'Oh, yes, that pink outfit.'

'Yeah, anyway I gave it to him. He was covered in dirt, and stuff. I don't know why, but I thought he was going to use it, to clean himself up with, but he took it, and ran off giggling.'

'It's probably, Trae and Octavius, up to their boyish ways. It's so nice how they've bonded' Aaronn mused.

'I can't believe, Melonhead is coming out here to see us all.' Octavius walked into the office. 'Do I look alright?'

'You look fine' Sloane reassured him. 'Anyway, the last thing I saw was Trae jumping into a pink convertible.'

'Oh, good' Octavius adjusted his scarf 'he got my present.'

'You bought Trae a pink convertible?' Aaronn choked on the laughter he tried to stem.

'No, I just ordered it.' Octavius chuckled 'on his card. Looks like it was finally, delivered.'

Aaronn looked at Sloane who shrugged. 'And how did you do that?'

'Easy.' Octavius looked at them and feigned a guilty look. 'Okay, I may have accidentally, looked at his credit card, and recorded his number, when he wasn't looking.'

'And' Aaronn stood with his arms folded across his chest, his foot tapped the floor, the only sign of his agitation.'

'And it was so simple, and maybe I accessed his computer. You were right, Sloane, people are stupid.'

'Huh!' Sloane shrugged and looked at Aaronn confused.

'I remembered that you were telling me that people use passwords that were simple to guess, and you told me some, remember.'

Sloane hit her forehead with the palm of her hand. 'I don't believe you remembered that.'

'Anyway, I tried them out. Let's see I tried – qwerty, qwerty1, abc123, password – but what let me in was 12345' Octavius laughed.

'Octavius, that's identity theft.' Aaronn shook his head in disbelief. *Oh, why should this surprise me?*

'Really' Octavius adjusted his fedora 'guess I don't know any better. After all, I'm just an octopus. But enough about Trae; have you noticed?' Octavius turned around in a circle. 'What do you think?'

Aaronn looked puzzled 'About what?'

'Well, I finally made a decision.' Octavius looked in the mirror 'I stuck a feather in my hat.'

'That's the decision you've been wrestling with for the last few months' Aaronn stood up and faced Octavius, incredulously.

'It's an important decision, Aaronn, and one I don't take lightly. Not everyone can get away with wearing a fedora, let alone one with feathers. So?'

'It looks really good' Sloane complimented him.

'Oh, you're just saying that because you know I'll murder you.' Octavius looked around the office as they laughed. 'So, where's the traitor?'

'We don't know' Aaronn picked up the car keys 'but we can't wait for Trae any longer.'

'Maybe he wants to arrive in his new car.' Octavius walked in front of the others out of the temporary building, to where the cars were parked out front.

'I can't see that happening' Aaronn unlocked the doors 'get in.'

'They gave you another car?' Sloane sat in the back seat so Octavius could have the front.

'I'm on probation.' Aaronn started the engine 'I can't let anything happen to this one for five years.' He reversed, and then drove the short distance to the park, where they were to meet General Melon.

'They've done a great job.' Sloane looked at the men who were hard at work, clearing the rubble from the buildings. The bobcats lifted load after load, into the dump trucks. 'Won't be long, and we'll be able to start rebuilding.'

Aaronn pulled into one of the car parks that lined the park and checked his watch. *Fifteen minutes to go,* he hurried the others, out of the car, and led the way, to the crowd which had already gathered. Most were in their dress uniforms, waiting for the order to line up and be presented, for their service to the island, in detecting, and destroying an enemy attack.

The park was in full splendour. The lawn areas perfectly manicured. A sea of pink, purple, yellow, and orange flowers showed the beauty of the cactus garden, and the rose garden that lay on each side of the fountain. The beauty of the flowers caught the eye of anyone looking at them and detracted from the small fence surrounding the gardens which said 'Danger. Keep out.'

Aaronn's mobile buzzed in his pocket. He took it out, turned off the alarm, and shut it down. *Eleven a.m.* and as ordered, the trucks and bobcats cut their engines, after they first, had lowered their shovels, and the trucks that were empty tilted their trays, as though they were bowing, before General Melon, for when he passed by. Silence filled the air as people waited expectantly.

As they waited, a heavy engine noise filled the silence. They looked at each other and shrugged. 'Isn't all the machinery supposed to stop?' Sloane questioned Aaronn. He nodded but the noise grew louder. They looked in the direction of the noise, and down at the end of the path they could see the headlights, of a machine coming towards them.

As it drew nearer, they could make out that it was one of the bobcats. Finally, it stopped, near the people who were waiting in formation. 'General Melon' Aaronn walked forward and helped General Melon out of the bobcat. 'What happened to the limousine I sent you?'

'The darnedest thing happened to us on the way here.' General Melon saluted the people 'Some ugly lady in a pink convertible, smashed into us and drove off. We had no choice but to borrow the nearest vehicle. Of course, there was only room enough for me; the rest had to run behind.' General Melon looked behind him 'Here they come now, the unfit, lazy good for nothing...'

'Sir,' the leader puffed as the group caught up 'didn't you see us waving at you, and shooting in your general direction, trying to get your attention?'

'Nope, didn't hear a thing. Now, Aaronn, are we ready?'

'Nope!' Aaronn turned to the crowd and called out at the top of his voice 'Attention!' Everyone stood to attention and waited. Aaronn shook his head and sighed. He tried to keep his mind on what General Melon was doing, but he couldn't help but wonder about the pink convertible that nearly ran the general down. Octavius had just admitted he bought one with Trae's money, and he knew that there was no other pink convertible on the island, so it had to have been Trae. He sighed as he knew deep down this was going to involve more paperwork. All he could hope for was that Trae would stay away till the general was gone.

General Melon stood in front of them; then he walked up and down in front of them before stopping in front of them again. 'Men and women, first, let me say that you have done your country proud. To uncover and thwart an enemy attack deserves the promotion I will be giving you all. To protect the inhabitants of this island shows your ability to put yourselves on the line for your fellow islanders. Bravo. Brigadier Octavius step forward please.'

Octavius stepped forward. General Melon pinned a medal on his scarf and saluted him. 'Brigadier, you took on, and destroyed all the Evil Corporation Incorporated by yourself and-'

'What now?' said Aaronn as he heard as did the others, a screeching of tyres, in the distance.

'Run' general Melon ordered 'it's that ugly lady.' A pink convertible sped along the path towards them and slammed on the brakes. As people scattered, the car ran over Octavius's tentacle before flipping, and landing, with its front end sitting in the fountain, and its back end resting on the wall of the fountain. 'That person's been taking lessons from you, Sloane.' General Melon echoed the thoughts that were in Aaronn's head.

'Ow, ow my tentacle is broken.'

They watched as she clambered ungracefully out of the door and fell into the water. Standing up she climbed over the edge of the fountain, her dress and hat, a sodden mess as she tottered towards them, her high heels clicking with each step.

'My dress!' Sloane exclaimed.

'Trae?' Aaronn acknowledged although he wasn't quite sure. As the person neared, they realised that 'she', was actually a 'he'. That their fears; were in fact a reality. Trae had lost the plot.

'General Melon' Trae saluted the general.

'Trae, you're out of uniform' General Melon saluted him back 'and you're wet.'

'Yes sir, yes, I am. I want out of this nuthouse.'

'Ow, ow, ow. What about me? You broke my tentacle. Medic-'

'You don't have bones in your tentacle, so it can't be broken' Trae muttered.

'I thought you said you weren't a marine biologist.' Octavius tilted his fedora to one side.

'I'm not. I thought you were injured.'

'Oh yeah, ow, my tentacle, medic, is there a medic here? I need a medic, and one that isn't Trae.'

Two men rushed over to Octavius. 'What do we do?' one of them said to the other.

'Let's massage the airways in his gills.'

'Don't even think about it.' Octavius took a step backwards 'You two are worse than Trae, and that's saying something.'

'I'll bandage it up for you, sir' the younger of the two said before taking Octavius's tentacle and bandaging it up.

'I can't believe you ran over me, Trae' Octavius moved his bandaged tentacle about.

'I can't believe you're still alive' Trae countered.

'Did you hear that?' Octavius spoke to all who were within earshot. 'Indignity after indignity, and after all I've done for you.'

'So,' General Melon turned his attention to Trae 'what has happened to you?'

'Me?!' He' Trae pointed to Octavius 'is a murdering lunatic.'

'Why are you dressed like a girl, Trae?'

'General Melon, I want out.'

'Not dressed like that you won't.' General Melon looked Trae up and down 'we don't do that anymore. We are more progressive remember. If you want to wear a dress, that's okay by us. By the way I forgot to note your gender. I'll mark you as female.'

'But I'm a male' Trae implored.

'Not anymore' General Melon handed a pen and some paperwork to Octavius to sign 'It's official now that a high-ranking officer has signed it.'

'That's right, Princess Rosie Alabaster Moonbeam' Octavius cackled 'I found your birth certificate when I was looking at your credit card. Oh yes, I know your real name, and now, so does everyone else' said Octavius with a smug look on his face, as laughter erupted from the crowd.

Trae's face went bright red, as General Melon continued 'Now, that it's official, why did you disrupt the service. I was about to give everyone a promotion?'

'My tentacle!' wailed Octavius.

'A promotion?! What for?' Trae stood with his hands on his hips. 'Octavius has shot me down, tied me up, tried to drown me, and he made me eat the chef-'

'The chef' General Melon looked around 'that's who's missing. He made the best fingers. I was looking forward to eating some while I was here.'

'Trae ate the last one' Octavius cackled.

'Why you-' Trae looked at everyone that was staring at him. 'What?! Octavius is not a war hero; he's an evil murderer ... and an octopus!' An audible gasp rippled through the crowd. Trae looked at the expressions of horror on their faces. 'Finally, I'm getting through to you idiots.'

The people turned on Trae and with one voice exclaimed 'You can't treat Octavius like that! He's a hero!' They gathered around Octavius and cheered him. Two men hoisted Octavius up, and onto their shoulders, while the people cheered. Trae stood and watched in disbelief, as Octavius waved to the crowd that adored him.

'What kind of nut house is this?!' Trae pushed his way through the crowd to the men who were shouldering Octavius. He grabbed Octavius by a couple of his tentacles and pulled him down to the ground.

In front of everyone, Trae grabbed Octavius's fedora, threw it onto the ground in frustration, stomped on it a few times, and screamed. 'HE'S AN OCTOPUS! - NOTHING BUT A PSYCHOTIC, MURDEROUS OCTOPUS! HE SHOULD BE FRIED IN LOTS OF OIL!' Trae stopped his rant, as he heard the audible gasps in the crowd. 'What? Like, none of you have thought of it!'

Trae stared at the crowd who were all staring at him. A few turned to Octavius and reassured him to ignore Trae's rant. 'I can't believe this!' Trae clenched his fist and bit his fingers. 'You're all insane, do you hear me, insane!' No one spoke, they just stared at him. 'What? I'm not the crazy one!'

'So says the man wearing a dress' Octavius mocked as he bent down to retrieve his fedora.

Trae shoved Octavius to one side. 'Oh, no you don't' he jumped up and down on the hat. 'You will not wear this again.' Trae stopped jumping, took a deep breath, and broke into song. 'I'm Octavius, a war hero / indignity after indignity. Someone cut me off / indignity after indignity. I treat everyone the same / indignity after indignity.'

Standing on one leg he lifted the other one up, and down on the fedora as he tried to squash it beyond recognition. 'I hate this fedora! I hate this island! I hate these people! But most of all, I hate you!'

'Oh, that's it!' Octavius picked Trae up and threw him as hard as he could, then he picked up his fedora, and set about trying to unflatten it. Trae screamed as he flew through the air. His screams turned from fear to agony as he landed in the cactus patch.

'Aaronn, what's going on?' General Melon demanded.

'It's a long story, general.'

'Mmm, I think I'll have an inquest.'

'What?' Aaronn looked at General Melon 'now.'

'Well, after we get Trae to hospital. Has anyone called the ambulance yet?'

As no one had Aaronn made the call as they walked over to where Trae was lying on his stomach, unconscious, his rear end full of cactus needles. They looked at Trae, and then each other, and burst out laughing.

'We shouldn't laugh at Trae.' Sloane wiped a tear from her eyes' she was laughing so much 'He won't be able to sit for weeks.'

'I don't think he's got that much sick leave left.' Aaronn mentally calculated Trae's days off as he started to stir.

'Well, this is a bit of a prickly situation' General Melon laughed at his own joke and continued. 'You could say that Octavius is a thorn in Trae's side.' Everyone continued laughing; they knew where this was going. 'In fact, we need a medic to remove the spines.' General Melon paused then continued 'You know, this is going to sting his pride.'

'Sharp one, Sir.' Octavius slapped General Melon who kept giggling, on the back.

Trae didn't look at them; he kept his face lowered to the ground, his insides cringing with every comment.

'You might say we're stabbing the drama.' General Melon: a five-star General in comedy. 'Don't think that

I don't have a point' the general continued. 'Wait for it, here's the stinger.'

They all stood in silence and looked at each other. Finally, Aaronn broke the silence 'Which is?'

'Can't quite put my finger on it?'

Trae groaned out loud. He'd heard enough. *Thank goodness* the siren of the ambulance got louder as it got closer, and switched off just before they stopped near Trae.

'Here's the ambulance' General Melon announced. 'So, how are you feeling, son, I mean daughter, hedgehog, uh whatever you are.'

'Kill me now' Trae moaned as the stretcher was put into the ambulance.

The ambulance officer slammed the back door shut with one of them inside to monitor Trae. He walked around to the driver's door, and went to get in. Octavius pulled the driver out and sat in the driver's seat. 'Trae wants to die, no one is driving but me, I'll make sure he dies.'

'Shove over' Sloane said pushing Octavius to the passenger seat 'I'll drive. I'll get him there fast, and alive.' As she started to leave Aaronn and General Melon squashed, themselves, into the front of the ambulance. Sloane accelerated. 'Get out of the car, there's not enough room for you lot.'

Aaronn grabbed the wheel 'You get out, you drive like a lunatic.' As Sloane and Aaronn, grappled with the wheel, each trying to wrench it from the other's hands, the ambulance veered from side to side.

'I'm telling you lot' General Melon grabbed the wheel to get everyone's attention. 'The answer is callisthenics. Lots of callisthenics, that'll burn off the weight. So, I think we should all support Trae, because that girl needs to shift some weight, and do callisthenics every morning. What do you think?'

'Not the time to discuss this, Sir.' Aaronn forced General Melon's hand off the wheel. 'Sloane give it up and let me drive. We're nearly there.' Aaronn pushed her closer to the door.

Octavius reached passed them all with one of his tentacles and opened the door. Sloane fell out as she was pushed up against it. With his free tentacles Octavius pushed both Aaronn, and General Melon out of the ambulance, and took control of the ambulance.

General Melon, Aaronn and Sloane picked themselves up off the ground. Sloane ran to a nearby car and hot-wired it. She stopped long enough to pick up General Melon and Aaronn, before taking off after the ambulance.

Outside of the hospital, two men in black, because they weren't suspicious enough, they had to wear black. On their sleeve a purple insignia - an upside down kite triangle with an eye in the middle, and a snake wrapped around it.

Evil Corporation Incorporated – the last survivors stood surveying their target. 'So, Magnus, it looks like our worthless mole and some equally worthless fodder died off. Predictable. Good help is hard to come by. Heh, good thing they were just bait to test the defences of this island.'

'I just don't see why they keep this island a secret, Tupin. I mean all they've managed to do, instead of letting other countries dispute for the territory, is enable corporations to swoop in, and become their own little nations.'

'Whatever the reason, I'm gonna blow those stupid little secret soldiers up, and their stupid little van, a get paid for it.' Tupin raised the rocket launcher he carried and aimed it at the hospital. 'But first some target practice.'

'Now!' Magnus yelled. A high-pitched screeching noise filled the air. 'Huh?'

Magnus and Tupin watched as an ambulance came flying around the corner, it hit a bump in the road, launched into the air, and crashed into the side of the hospital.

'What the ...?' Tupin lowered the rocket launcher.

'Did you see that, or do I need a vacation?' Magnus stared open mouthed, as the back of the ambulance back door flew open, and a stretcher fell out and started to roll towards them. 'Would you look at that? A car with three people chasing an ambulance, driven by a fedora wearing octopus, that steered the ambulance – which we were going to destroy to make it look like an explosion.'

'Yeah. That.' Tupin scratched his head 'We don't need to do anything; they seem to be quite capable of killing themselves without us.'

'Saw it, and still want a vacation. Maybe, somewhere safe; like that new grenadeball stadium on the other side of the island. Are you coming, Tupin?'

Trae screamed as his stretcher came to a stop in front of the two Evil Corporation Incorporated. General Melon, and the others ran up to Trae. Octavius reached the group last, took one look at the athletic figure holding the rocket launcher. 'See, Trae, fit.'

'I concur' General Melon began warming up exercises 'now everyone, time for star jumps! Take your positions and -'

'I'm strapped to this stretcher.'

'You use any excuse to get out of exercise, Trae.' General Melon started doing push ups.

As Octavius limbered up, he looked at the two Evil Corporation Incorporated standing there confused. 'Typical: Trae, even injured, you still manage to contact your allies.'

Magnus and Tupin watched them doing their exercises, shook their heads in disgust and pushed Trae's stretcher through the front doors of the hospital, rang the bell and walked out. 'How about we go watch the sun set?' Tupin asked as he held Magnus's hand.

As they walked off, they saw General Melon doing sit ups with the rest of the team groaning as they did their sit ups, and the strange talking octopus doing what appeared to be push ups with all eight tentacles.'

'Indignity after indignity' Octavius complained.

Hand in hand the two men continued to walk off into the sunset.

*** XI ***

Trae thought he had heard all the jokes from his so-called friends, but no the doctors and nurses were no better. Joke after joke as they removed the needles. He lay on his stomach, his face red with humiliation. *At least the pain killers numbed the pain I'm in. Shame they couldn't numb my brain.* Trae groaned. *Thank goodness I've banned all visitors. When I get out of here, I need to check Sloane's phone. I think she took another photo. I don't want that one on the net.* He closed his eyes to try and get some sleep.

'Go away' Trae muttered as he felt something poking his forehead. He slowly opened his sleep-filled eyes. 'Aarrgh' he involuntarily screamed as he saw Octavius's face staring at him.

'The cry of the guilty' Octavius attached himself to Trae.

'Or' Aaronn peeled Octavius off Trae's face 'it could just be your ugly mug.'

'Melon, Aaronn's being mean again. Did you know he killed our receptionist?'

'What?' General Melon pondered for a moment 'that's it; we're having that inquest now.'

'Go away!' Trae pushed the buzzer to alert the nurse. *What was taking her so long?* He kept pushing the buzzer.

'Okay, okay, calm down, Trae.' Aaronn removed the buzzer from Trae's hand 'Besides we told the nurse to ignore the buzzer.'

'What? You can't do that. What about my-'

'All right you lot. Take a seat.' General Melon started to move the chairs that were in the room for visitors, around Trae's bed in a half circle. Sloane took the first seat, and wiped her forehead with a towel, that she had found in the ensuite of Trae's room. Aaronn sat next to her, and Octavius sat next to Aaronn.

Trae raised his head and looked at them. *I can't believe this. Fancy holding an inquest in a hospital – who does that?* Trae wrinkled his nose in disgust as an unpleasant odour hit him. 'What is that stench?'

Octavius lifted one of his tentacles up and sniffed where it attached to his body. Then he leaned over to Aaronn and sniffed his armpit. 'Aaronn, it's Aaronn who stinks. Must be the exercise regime we just did.'

'That's right' General Melon crouched down next to Octavius. 'I've decided to get you lot moving, get you fit, so it's callisthenics every morning.'

Trae groaned. Sloane shook her head as she looked at Trae. 'I can't believe you've let yourself go so much, Trae. You not only ruined my dress, but now I have to exercise.'

'Yeah, Trae' Octavius leaned forward, and looked at him 'it's all, your fault that we now have to exercise. You've put on way too much weight.'

'It's not fat, it's soft muscle' Trae said forlornly.

'No, I'm pretty sure I saw it moving.' Sloane sighed 'You got fat. Admit it.'

'And that's why as soon as you're out of hospital you can join us. Nothing beats an hour of push ups, star jumps, and sit ups. It's invigorating.' General Melon pulled another chair into the half circle. He moved Aaronn to the new seat while he took the now empty seat that was in front of Trae and pulled out a small whiteboard.

'Where did you get that whiteboard, sir' asked Aaronn.

'Oh, when I was walking in here, I realised I'd need something to write on. As I was passing the nurses' desk, I saw it propped up. It just had some notes about one of the patients, so I borrowed it.'

'But what about the patient?' Aaronn said, 'they might have needed those notes.'

'Good point, Aaronn, but too late, the deed is done. Now Trae' General Melon handed Trae a white board marker 'I want you to write down a list of what you think has happened.'

Trae stretched out his arm to the whiteboard. 'I'll write small, I don't think there's enough room otherwise.'

'Very well, begin.' General Melon held the board with a vice like grip, so it didn't move as Trae wrote on it.

'Well, it all started when Octavius shot down my helicopter, and killed everyone except for me, and another person.' Trae spoke as he wrote on the board.

'Innocent, I tell you!' Octavius yelled out 'you killed them not me.'

'Aaronn' General Melon looked from Trae to Octavius 'clarify!'

'We were playing grenadeball, sir, and it flew into the chopper. Trae kicked it into the cockpit, and it exploded.'

'It's just the stupidest game ever played. Who on earth plays with a live grenade with the pin pulled?' Trae complained as he went to write on the board, the next incident.

'C'mon, Melonhead' Octavius goaded 'you're not entirely impartial to a little game of grenadeball.'

General Melon laughed. 'That's right you little squirt. I'm the one who taught you.'

'But that's so reckless' Trae said incredulously.

'Well, yes, and no. Normally we use flash bangs, Trae, you know for safety reasons, but occasionally we use the real deal, and I am pretty fast. It's a great stress relief game, and you, Trae, sound like you need to relax.' General Melon tapped the whiteboard 'Carry on.'

Trae began to write. 'So, then Octavius tried to drown me, I was arrested, my computer was bugged, Octavius sent pizzas to me all night long, then he destroyed the supermarket, and nearly ran over us with a tank, but he did run over a civilian, then I had to deal with the passengers of a plane that Octavius shot down.

If that wasn't bad enough, he killed the chef, and made me and Aaronn eat him, the Evil Corporation Incorporated showed up, caused a lot of trouble, we fought them, well, Octavius fought them, oh, and he tied me up, but anyway, they were all killed except the two I just saw at the hospital. Then Octavius shot me in the foot, and someone ordered a pink convertible in my name, and I'm guessing that was Octavius's handiwork too. And then, he threw me into a cactus plant.' *Where's the nurse with my pain killers?* Trae groaned as a stab of pain hit him.'

'Whinge, whinge, whinge' Octavius cut in 'do you hear me complaining? No. And I have a broken tentacle. And after all I've done for you. Indignity after indignity!'

General Melon stood and turned the whiteboard around to face him. 'Is this true, Aaronn?'

'It's more or less correct. It has been a lot more involved than that.'

'Sloane' General Melon looked in her direction.

'I came in after the drowning incident, but pretty much it is correct.'

'Octavius, what have you, got to say for yourself?' General Melon studied what was written on the board.

'I don't know why I'm being picked on sir. I have treated, Trae the same as I treat everyone, and I think, that if you look at things from my perspective-'

'-That's a load of rubbish!' Trae cut Octavius off, mid-sentence.

'All right!' General Melon picked up the eraser. 'Well, I'm dismissing the first event, Trae. You can't blame Octavius for downing the chopper, and people being killed, when you are the one, who kicked the grenade, into the cockpit. Now do you want that against your record?'

'Will it get me off the island?'

'No, Trae, it won't. But you will get a frowny face on your record.' General Melon erased the incident off the whiteboard. 'Now as for the drowning incident – I'm certain that was just a misunderstanding. I'm sure the brigadier didn't want you dead, did you Octavius?'

'No, sir, I was just interrogating the traitor.'

'There you are. See, Trae, you misunderstood. He was simply interrogating you.'

'But I'm not a traitor.'

'Keep telling yourself that' Octavius whispered to Trae 'and you might believe it one day.'

'You should be thanking Octavius' General Melon ignored the choking sound Trae made 'after all, if it weren't for his paranoia, the Evil Corporation Incorporated would not have been discovered, till it was too late.'

I can't believe this Trae watched as General Melon erased every incident after explaining it away with some inane logic. *How can Octavius cause so much trouble yet come out looking like the hero. Unbelievable!*

'I would say, Trae, from my observations' General Melon leaned against the edge of the table 'you have had some major problems adjusting to life on this island. Out of all your complaints the only one that seems to be serious...'

Are you kidding? Trae stared at the general, who kept talking *there's only one serious incident.*

'So, Octavius' General Melon questioned 'this incident with the chef.'

'What about it?' Octavius waved his bandaged tentacle about.

Did you kill the chef?'

'Yes, what are you going to do about it?' Octavius challenged General Melon. 'It was me or him.'

'Are you saying that you acted in self-defence?'

'Sure, Melonhead, he looked at me the wrong way – with hungry eyes.'

'In that case, Octavius' General Melon took a notebook out of his pocket 'we'll write an official letter to his family, and say he was a casualty of war, or something.'

'I've already sent one' Sloane checked her notebook 'yep, already done.'

'Good, good' General Melon put his notebook away 'this inquest is now finished.'

'You can't do that, general.' Trae winced from the pain. 'Octavius is a cold-blooded killer. He should be dealt with! Somehow, there has to be a way!'

'I don't know what I've done for you to say that' Octavius squatted down in front of Trae and looked at him. 'You heard Melonhead. You misunderstand everything I do and say.' Octavius stood up and swiped Trae across his posterior.

'Ow, you ...' Trae bit of the expletive he was going to utter. *Pain, the pain, I'm going to kill him.*

'Trae' General Melon interjected 'I think you need a holiday. I'll arrange it.'

'Yes sir, thank you, sir.' *Finally,* Trae watched them all leave. *Now, maybe I can get some peace.*

'Oh no' Sloane jerked her head towards the door 'can anyone else hear that?'

'What, the Carollers?' Aaronn said.

'No' Sloane got up 'the gunshots and screaming.'

Why did they look so scared? Aaronn, Sloane, and General Melon, why did they look so scared, they weren't afraid of anything. Trae looked in the direction of the doorway. He watched as doctors, nurses and patients ran through the corridor, yelling and screaming. Some of the patients used their crutches or wheelchairs to force their way through. *What is going on?*

A nurse stumbled her way to the doorway, she held one hand on her stomach in a vain attempt to stop the blood that was seeping out. 'Run' she gasped, as she collapsed to the floor 'he's here.'

Through the intercom system came the wailing of a siren. 'Attention ... attention' the voice on the intercom system started 'this is an emergency. It's Christmas.

You're on your own, good luck.' The wailing of the siren continued for another minute then stopped.

'We have to go' Sloane started to run to the door.

'What about me? What's happening?' Trae asked panicking.

'Didn't you hear the broadcast? You're on your own.' Sloane said as she unsuccessfully tried to get through the people panicking. 'Santa's here. Octavius, a little help if you don't mind!'

'The things I do for you, and not a thank you do I get' Octavius hurried the door 'now when I stop them, run for it.' He held onto the door edge, and threw his body out, with his tentacles stretched out wide, hitting people in the face, which stopped them mid run.

'Wait' Trae called out as they all ran out of the room. *Why did they look so scared? Hang on it's only August, it's not Christmas time yet. My head hurts.* He rested his head on his folded arms.

'Ho, Ho, Ho'

Trae raised his head to look at who spoke. 'Santa?' *This can't be Santa. This can't be real. I'm hallucinating, that is the only logical answer.*

'Ho, Ho, Ho, who's been a naughty boy, Trae' Santa took a puff from his cigar.

'I didn't know you smoked' Trae looked at Santa. *Then again, he's skinny, not at all fat, like the ones' I've seen, and is that a machine gun hanging around his neck.* 'You can't be Santa, and it's nowhere near Christmas time. This is a joke, right? Right?'

'Ho, Ho, Ho' Santa blew smoke rings 'I'm the real Santa, and this is the true time of Christmas. Santa turned towards the doorway, raised the machine gun and let off a blast, at the screaming people who were running past. A few bodies fell, and the rest of the people screamed louder, some trampled over the bodies, and others tried unsuccessfully to turn and run back the way they had come in their panic. He turned back to Trae 'And this is no joke. I take my job very seriously.'

'But the gun.'

'All the better to shoot you with, Trae. You've been a very bad boy, Ho, Ho, Ho.'

'Noooo!' Someone help me.'

'There you are Santa' Octavius stood behind Santa holding a knife 'I've been looking everywhere for you. I should've known you'd be here.'

'Octavius, Ho, Ho, Ho' Santa pointed the gun at him 'you've been a very naughty-'

'I know' Octavius plunged the knife through Santa's heart before he could let a shot off. 'Yes, I finally got you first this year. I win' Octavius declared over Santa's slumped body, which had fallen, with his hand stretched out towards Trae.

As Santa fell to the floor, his blood seeping out and forming into a pool. Trae screamed. Octavius pulled the knife out, and shoved it in Trae's hand, just as a nurse came running in. She saw the knife in Trae's hand, and Santa pointing in his direction. 'You've killed, Santa.' She checked Santa's pulse briefly. 'He's dead!' She screamed 'HE'S DEAD! SANTA'S DEAD!'

A calmness came over the building as people heard the news and stopped panicking. As other nurses and doctors came into the room. The nurse pointed at Trae 'He killed Santa! One of the doctors knelt down next to Trae and whispered 'Well done, but this is how Santa behaved. We were used to this happening every year.'

The nurse looked at Trae with disgust 'You have killed Christmas.

'What?! No, I didn't' Trae dropped the knife on the floor 'I couldn't, it was Octavius.'

'Oh, that's right, blame me. You have just killed Christmas, Trae.'

'Quick get a stretcher' a doctor yelled 'I think I have a pulse.'

'It's too late' a nurse yelled 'you don't want to save this one.'

Octavius watched the doctor and nurse argue about whether or not to save Santa. As they removed Santa's body, Octavius walked out of the room whistling.

How does he do that? Trae fell back to sleep. 'Ow' Trae saw a nurse holding a needle. *Now you give me the pain medication.* He yawned and could feel his eyes closing. *All this stress is not good for me. Maybe when I wake up, this will have been just a dream. That's it, just a horrible, horrible dream.* Now that the noise had died down, and as he started to go to sleep, he could hear the carolers still singing, from outside of his window. *And still they sing.*

*** XII ***

Trae was released from hospital after two weeks. True to his word, General Melon had arranged for his break. *Maybe General Melon was right* he shut the lid of his suitcase. *Maybe all I need is a break, and to think about my options. Do I want to stay in the army, and be stuck on this island with a psychotic octopus, or leave the only life I know?* 'But then, will I be able to leave anyway? Aaronn keeps telling me that once you're on the island, you can't leave. This is not what I signed up for when I transferred.*

Trae was picked up a short time later and taken to the landing strip where a small plane was waiting for him. Trae half laughed, some *landing strip. It was nothing but a sandy strip that led to the sea, that was lined with palm trees. It was the same strip that he crashed into when he first arrived. Well, maybe if I'm lucky, I'll crash, again.*

Back to where it all began. He walked up the steps and was shown to his seat. 'We're just waiting for one more passenger and then we will leave' the steward informed him. 'Would you like a tea or coffee after take-off?'

'A tea would be nice' Trae responded and settled into his seat. He closed his eyes and felt the tension starting to leave him. The engines roared into life. *Soon I'll be free.*

'Boy, I'm so glad they waited for me.' The voice jarred every nerve. Trae opened his eyes, and found himself, staring at Octavius 'Melonhead said that I needed a break too.'

'NOOOOOOOO!' he screamed as the plane took off.

'Wow, that boy sure can scream' General Melon said to Aaronn and Sloane, who were there to make sure they left.

'That he can, Sir' Aaronn agreed 'that he can.'

'Wanna take bets as to whether they both return, or just Octavius?' Sloane took out her pen and paper to write down their bets.

'I'll go the risky route.' Aaronn thought for a moment and then laughed quietly. 'Yeah, how about, Trae survives, and Octavius comes back either crippled or dead. Oh, and Trae comes running back, screaming, being chased by some angry faction.'

'I like it, but they will both be back.' General Melon emptied out his rifle and put the magazine in the bag that held the grenades. 'Grenadeball anyone?' he held out the rifle. Sloane and Aaronn shrugged and took their positions.

'So, where's the plane going?' asked Sloane, who wrote down her bet.

'Heh heh' General Melon laughed 'the other side of the island.'

'That's unfair, sir.' Sloane tore the page out of her notebook 'You have insider information, bets are off.'

'No, they're not.' General Melon grabbed his rifle by the barrel. 'Tribal laws, I'm the chief, and the bets are still on.' He handed Aaronn a grenade. 'Go for it boy. Toss it to me. Sloane, go catch.'

'Hang on, sir. Isn't Octavius already crippled, and they're both coming back? Doesn't that mean I already win?' I know Trae isn't being chased by anyone yet, but it's Trae, we know at some point some angry person, or faction will chase him.'

They looked at Aaronn in astonishment that he had already won the bet. True, they still didn't know if they would make it back, but as they were only going to the other side of the island, it did seem that, Aaronn had indeed won the bet.

'Drats, beaten by my own rules.' General Melon threw his rifle down on the ground, which somehow discharged. 'How did you get that right, so quickly?'

'Sir, your leg is bleeding.' Aaronn noticed a dark patch appearing on General Melon's trouser leg.

General Melon looked at his leg. 'And our medic is on vacation. Oh well' he shrugged and picked up his rifle ready to bat. 'Oops, I nearly forgot, I'm opening the new grenadeball stadium today.'

'Sir?' Aaronn looked at Sloane who just shrugged.

'I'm sure we'll meet Trae over there, and he can patch my leg up.'

'We could also go to the hospital' Sloane helped General Melon as he limped towards the car.

'No, no Trae's the medic, he can fix it.' General Melon got in the back seat so he could rest his leg. 'That's an order, Aaronn. Let's go, you're driving.'

'I don't know why people don't like my driving" Sloane complained as she got in the front passenger seat.

'About time you stopped screaming' Octavius nudged Trae 'I can't believe you brought your buddies along for the ride.'

'What are you talking about, Octavius?' Trae tried to control his breathing. *Why? Why can't I get a break from Octavius?'*

'Those two guys behind us' Octavius dropped his voice to a whisper 'they're the Evil Corporation Incorporated who were at the hospital.'

'Don't be silly, Octavius.'

'I'm not; they have the Evil Corporation Incorporated insignia on their sleeve.'

'What are they doing on our flight?'

Octavius stood up to ask them, but as he did so, the captain, wearing a parachute, walked down the aisle.

Trae looked at the captain. 'You're Robert! What are you doing here, you can't fly a plane?'

'I know, I'm a kangaroo, doesn't anyone know my name? Besides, being a pilot is not the job for me. Look at my tiny hand paws, they're ridiculously cute, but useless. I'll never know why I keep getting these jobs. I should be in a zoo. Being a pilot is not the job for me.' *Boing, Boing, Boing* Rodney hopped down the plane to the exit door, opened it and jumped out.

The two members of The Evil Corporation Incorporated ran to the back of the plane, grabbed a parachute each from the holder, and put it on. 'What do you think you're doing?' Trae yelled. *I can't believe I'm going to die.*

'Getting away from you two?' one of The Evil Corporation Incorporated tightened the strap of the parachute 'people get hurt around you.'

'Noooo' Trae screamed, and looked at Octavius 'What do we do? What do we do? We have no pilot.'

'Well, there's no parachutes left, I guess we'll have to learn how to fly' Octavius threw Trae out, and jumped out after them, and began to free fall to the earth.

As they plummeted towards the ground Octavius, holding onto his fedora with one tentacle, and Trae, who was screaming, reached out as they passed by the Evil Corporation Incorporated, who had activated their parachutes, and grabbed hold of their legs. Octavius on one, and Trae on the other. 'Get off of us!' Tupin yelled as they tried to shake off Octavius and Trae without success.

'No!' Trae screamed 'I'm too young to die.'

'If you don't look down, Trae' Octavius yelled 'it's a fun ride!'

'Here we are sir' Aaronn stopped the car outside of the huge unmistakable yellow hive-shaped structure of the new grenadeball stadium.

'I still can't believe they painted it yellow' Sloane stretched, 'What's all that noise?' she asked as they walked past the two cacti that were guarding the front door.

As they walked inside, they could see that the crowd there was cheering and screaming. They looked at the big screen which highlighted the action and gave close ups of what happens in the main arena.

'Thank you, thank you' the camera panned a close up of the Demon Washing Machine 'I promise that if you vote me as the island's chieftain in the next election, I won't kill you, you lowly peasants. Well maybe some.'

'It looks like you have competition this year, sir' Aaronn said. He turned to Sloane 'I still don't know how you made that thing come alive.'

'You were there, all I did was turn it on, but when I turned it off, it disconnected itself, and walked out of the door and it's been threatening us with destruction ever since.'

'You don't want to vote for the same old, geriatric that you have for the last – forever' the demon washing machine continued.

'Hey, who's he calling old' General Melon said to Sloane.

'I don't know, sir. You're fitter than most people here.'

'My pledge to you is this.' the Demon Washing Machine laughed 'I promise to tyrannise you, and treat you like the dirt under my feet that you are, and if you obey my every direction, I will let you live.'

As They walked down the aisle to the centre of the ring, General Melon looked at the screen 'I can't believe the audacity of that machine. There's to be no advertising in my stadium, except for mine.'

'Hey look' Aaronn pointed up at the sky as they walked into the ring so that General Melon could confront the demon washing machine 'up there.'

'Hey! It looks like we're going to land in the grenadeball stadium!' Octavius yelled 'This is awesome, we'll have an audience. Make it look good, Trae! It looks like a huge crowd is watching the game!'

Octavius was the first to land, he timed his move perfectly, so that just before he landed, he let go of the Evil Corporation Incorporated leg, and still holding onto his fedora, curled up into a ball, rolled to one side as the person that he was hitching a ride on landed, and ran a few steps while the parachute dropped behind him. Octavius then stood up and bowed as the crowd erupted into a cheer.

Make it look good he said. It's fun, he said. Trae was sure he was going to throw up. *This isn't fun, Octavius.* Trae tried to judge his landing. *Concentrate. Concentrate.* Just as Trae was about to land, Octavius yelled out 'Make it look good, Trae!'

Trae distracted by Octavius tripped as he hit the ground, a gust of wind blew through dragging the parachute further than it should. As Trae was dragged along the ground because he had not let go of the Evil Corporation Incorporated leg, he heard Octavius say, 'I'll help you, Trae.'

How are you going to help m- He felt his trousers rip slightly as they were pulled down towards his ankles. *Aarrgh I should've worn a belt. I can't believe Octavius pulled my trousers down. Oh well, it's a good thing that I'm wearing my boxer shorts although they are a bit on the tight side.*

A shade of red flushed through Trae's body as he remembered that the boxers, he had put on that morning were red with bright pink love hearts on them and trimmed with white lace. *The shame* Trae stood up in the middle of the stadium as everyone looked at him stunned in silence.

'Well, someone has to love him' Octavius broke the silence 'he might as well love himself.'

The crowd roared with laughter at Trae and cheered for the upcoming the game.

The two members of the Evil Corporation Incorporated were rolling up their parachutes as something came flying into the stadium. 'Run' Octavius yelled as he ran for the exit. Trae tried to run and found himself falling as he ran; the idea to pull his trousers up didn't enter his head. The fallout from a loud explosion behind him propelled him forward and he fell, face first into the dirt floor.

The crowd erupted into cheers and applause when the smoke and dirt settled and showed that the Evil Corporation Incorporated had been destroyed.

What's that? Trae noticed an object near them. 'Aarrgh, a grenade.'

'That's a phosperous grenade' Aaronn stated 'get rid of it, Trae. Toss it.'

The audience began to make a hasty exit when they saw Trae playing with the grenade. Trae grabbed it and tossed it at Aaronn. 'I don't want it, you idiot' Aaronn tossed it at General Melon.

'Ooh, hot potato ... Your turn, Sloane' he tossed it to her.

'I don't want it' she ran over to the Demon Washing Machine, and tossed it in.

'Arrgh, I don't want it; I'm meant to make you suffer. Help me, someone help me.'

'With pleasure' Octavius grabbed the fire bucket of water, lifted the lid, and poured it into the machine.

'It burns, aarrgh. My circuits, it's burning me.'

'Everyone - run' General Melon shouted. They ran in different directions to find somewhere that was somewhat protective and had just taken cover when the Demon Washing Machine blew up.

'Trae' General Melon said as the air cleared 'you left in such a hurry you forgot to bandage my leg up.'

'I didn't know you were injured.'

'Shot myself in the leg' General Melon rolled up his trouser leg to show him.

'And you haven't got that treated yet?'

'Well, you're the medic.'

'But you run the risk of infection.' Trae took a look at general Melon's leg. *Unbelievable. What is Sloane laughing at?*

'Trae, pull your trousers up properly' Octavius ordered 'I've seen more of your flesh than I ever want to see again.'

Oh, that's what Sloane's laughing at. I don't even want to know what she thinks. 'No!' Trae tried to knock Sloane's mobile out of her hand 'no pictures!'

Aaronn looked at Trae trying to take the phone from Sloane 'Do I want to know what happened?'

'Well' Octavius began.

'Later' General Melon interrupted 'my leg.'

'Can you guys give us a lift' Trae asked bandaging the leg 'and stop at the hospital so he can get the bullet out.'

'Hey, Trae' Octavius said as they all got in the car. 'You know how I said to make your landing good.'

'Yes' Trae mentally steeled himself.

'That was spectacular' Octavius cackled.

*** XIII ***

Still stuck on this island, different day, same chaos. Trae sighed as he walked into Aaronn's office the following morning to discuss the previous day's events. 'Aaronn, I know I'm going to regret this' Trae sat down 'but what is Octavius doing? I just saw him standing on a table holding a lighted candle up to one off the smoke detectors.'

'He's checking to see if they work yet.'

'Huh!'

'It's quite simple, Trae. Now that the offices have been rebuilt, we have to have smoke alarms installed. It's the new building codes. They were put in yesterday and the electrician is coming back today to connect the last one, so they work. Octavius is doubling as the Occupational, Health and Safety officer, so he's checking them so that he can report they don't work.'

'That nut case is the safety officer. You have got to be kidding; he's a danger to, well, everyone!'

Aaronn and Trae looked at the door to see who had just knocked. Octavius came in holding his lighted candle. 'None of them work, Aaronn.' The lights went out for a few moments and then came on. 'I'll just check yours, but it's not looking good.' Octavius climbed up onto the table. As he climbed up, he slipped slightly on some papers that were on the table, steadying himself he stood up, and held the candle so the flame sat under the smoke and heat detector.'

'Shouldn't you just press the test button' Trae said shaking his head.

'What? Are you an electronics expert now?' Octavius looked at how far he was holding the candle under the fire alarm. 'This is more fun, and the more correct way to test it.'

'Says who?' Trae looked at Aaronn who just shrugged his shoulders.

'Says me, and I'm all that counts.' Suddenly the alarm went off and startled Octavius.

He slid off the desk and landed on the floor, the tentacle holding the candle outstretched towards Trae's leg. 'That wasn't meant to happen' Octavius let go off the candle and sat up. He reached out to pick up his fedora that had fallen off. 'Yuck, it's getting wet.'

'I guess the smoke detectors have finally been connected' Aaronn tried to pick up the papers on his desk to stop them getting wet. 'Will you get off the desk?' he gave Octavius a little shove.

'Indignity after indignity' Octavius got off the desk and looked at the sprinkler that had appeared 'They're working now, Aaronn.'

'You don't say.'

'What's that smell?' Trae looked down at the floor. 'Aarrgh! I'm on fire!' he stood up and tried to pat his trouser leg to put out the flame. He kicked Octavius out of the way, dropped to the floor and rolled.

'Oh, stop crying, Trae' Octavius said just as the sprinklers popped out from the ceiling, and started spraying water all over the office. "Look, the sprinklers are working. You'll be fine.'

'You set me on fire!' Trae lay on the floor soaked by the water, the fire now out.

'Well, you're not on fire now.'

'No thanks to you!' Trae clenched his teeth as he stood up 'Ow, this hurts.'

'I guess you want to go to the hospital, again' Octavius picked up Aaronn's car keys.

'Considering, I probably have third degree burns on my leg. Yes.'

'Whinge, whinge, whinge' Octavius walked to the door 'C'mon then, and you call yourself a medic.'

Trae bit back the reply as he limped after Octavius. Aaronn sighed as he looked at the sodden pieces of paper on his desk. He swallowed his coffee, and started to mop up the mess, now that the sprinklers had turned themselves off.

'Hello' he answered his phone that was ringing. *Oh, great the system triggered an alarm at the fire station.* 'No, there's no fire. You don't need to come out, just a small accident. Yes, it's good to know the system works.' He hung up the receiver. 'Don't ask' he noticed Sloane standing in the doorway 'give me a lift to the hospital. Octavius took my car keys.' Aaronn went to walk out of the room. 'Oh, all right' Aaronn couldn't stand the way Sloane was looking at him. 'I'll tell you on the way.'

'Trae has the worst luck' Sloane parked in the hospital's car park. As she turned the engine off one of the back doors fell off, and the boot flew open.

'Yeah' Aaronn said sarcastically as he looked at her car 'he has the worst luck.'

As they walked across towards the front doors, General Melon jogged up to them, and started jogging on the spot. 'Top of the morning people! What brings you here?'

'Trae had a slight accident' Aaronn began.

'Octavius set him on fire' Sloane corrected as she laughed.

'Oh, oh, I can see another incident report coming my way.' General Melon slowed down his jogging on the spot to a slow step and walked with them to the front doors. 'You have no idea the pile of reports he has sent me, but they are good for keeping the log fire burning at night.' The general laughed as the doors to the hospital flew open, and Octavius came running out.

'Oh, good you're here. I've lost Trae.'

'And that's a problem to you, how?' Aaronn rubbed his forehead.

'You don't understand. He ran out of the ward screaming "His kind must die" and then he disappeared. What do you think he meant, Aaron?'

Aaronn shrugged his shoulders. 'I don't know, but I'm sure he'll turn up. Let's go back to the office; I'm sure he can't get into too much trouble.'

'But the look in his eyes ...'

'Hey, look up there' General Melon pointed to the roof of the hospital 'Trae, is that you? You'd better come down here before you get hurt, again!'

'Not till you deal with that that thing!' Trae yelled as he threw a pair of shoes at Octavius.

'You wait right there' Octavius caught the shoes, and threw them back, as he took off into the hospital to get to the roof and deal with Trae.

'Quick' Sloane pulled her notebook out 'who's coming off the roof, Trae or Octavius?'

They all laughed, and she put her notebook away 'Yeah, that would've been a silly bet.' She looked up at the roof 'Oh, he's gone.'

'Did you see where he went?' Octavius hurried up to them 'he's disappeared again.'

'No' Sloane said, 'he hasn't come this way.'

'Well, I will find him, and when I do' Octavius slapped two of his tentacles together 'I'm going to-'

'Brigadier' Aaronn warned 'that's enough. Trae has obviously had a rough day. Give him his space, Octavius, this is Trae, he won't do anything else crazy.

*** XIV ***

Sloane and Octavius met Aaronn and General Melon in Aaronn's office. 'We stopped for pizza' Sloane explained when they walked into his office.

'That's not healthy, Sloane.' General Melon stood up and did a few squats 'You should have picked up some salad.'

'Well, you don't have to eat it, sir' Sloane put the boxes down on Aaronn's desk.

'True, but it'd be a shame to waste it.' General Melon picked up the TV remote and switched on the television. 'Nothing like a bit of TV, to go with the pizza, heh heh!'

They were laughing and talking as they ate the pizzas. Sloane and Aaronn were mid-bite when the newsflash came on. 'And news just in. The battleship Gulpin has been hijacked by a medic, by the name of Trae. He is armed and is considered dangerous. He has forced the crew of the Gulpin to jump ship and was last seen heading towards an unmanned oil rig.

The news reporter tapped his ear and shuffled his paperwork. As many of you may remember this man appeared at the opening ceremony where TV host and runner-up in the elections – the Demon Washing Machine made a guest appearance campaigning and was unfortunately injured in the sporting event. And playing behind me are some pictures of that event. There are lots of famous faces.' Images of Trae landing in the Grenadeball Stadium flashed across the screen. The camera panned back to the reporter 'And I've just been told that we have our best software engineers that aren't Sloane, attempting to fix the Demon Washing Machine, so that we have a fair election.'

'Hey, what's wrong with me? Sloane complained.

'Shush Sloane, this isn't about you' Aaronn said, 'now listen.'

'It has also come to our attention that this man, Trae, might've also have been responsible for the Christmas tragedy last month in August. He is also known to have a history of sleeping rough, harassing a decorated war hero, impulsive spending and has built up a reputation for being a public menace. And yes, we are going live to one of our reporters who is talking to Roscoe, I believe it is. George, can you hear us alright?'

'Yes, I can, and good afternoon to you all. I am here at the base, and I have with me here Raul, who has had some interactions with this Trae character.' The camera panned out so that Rodney came into view. 'So, Raul, tell us about your interactions with Trae.'

'Well, it's because of Trae that I have lost every job I was given. I know that I wasn't qualified to do them, but that is beside the point. Every time I lost my job, Trae was the root cause. And what's more, I am a kangaroo, what do you expect? I have short hands, see' Rodney waved his little kangaroo hands in front of the camera 'incredibly cute, but useless. And why can't anyone remember my name? Is it so hard to remember, Rodney?' Rodney hopped away.

'And there you have it; Trae got that poor chap fired from every job he had. Now we're just going to talk to these two chaps that I've just seen lurking around the hospital down here at the base. Excuse me' George went up to the two men.

'Yes, you two, who look a little shifty. Do you know anything about Trae? Hang on – weren't you two at the Grenadeball Stadium?'

'Yes, yes, we were, I'm Magnus'

'And I'm Tupin.'

'I thought you two died in the stadium.'

'No, we were injured pretty badly, but now we're on the mend,' said Magnus.

'Did you meet Trae at all during your stay here?' George asked.

'Yes' Magnus said 'when he first got here, he slept in the park and boy did he disturb the peace with his snoring.

Tupin nodded in agreement 'We even drew funny faces on him one night, and one night we covered him with leaves, and he didn't wake up. But we did feel sorry for him at one point, and we wheeled him into the hospital.'

'Yes, trouble does seem to follow Trae' Magnus said, 'now if you'll excuse us, we need to get back to work.'

'Oh no, Magnus look' Tupin pointed to Pain who was heading in their direction.

'Dr Pain' the reporter held the microphone out to Pain 'are you here to talk about Trae?'

'No, that boy is too soft, he refuses to hurt himself properly. I'm here because these two' Pain grabbed Magnus and Tupin by the back of their shirt, as they tried to walk away 'need some physiotherapy to heal quicker.' Pain pushed them to the ground and put his foot on Magnus's back 'Give me fifty push ups.'

'Get off my back.'

'No, you need resistance training, now push.'

'Well, thank you for your report gentlemen. We'll leave you to your therapy session.

George turned to the camera 'Now if you come over here with me, I have someone else who wants to say something.' The cameraman followed George as he walked over to a group of four males, and four females of various ages.

One member of the group stepped forward as George came up to them. 'And you are?' George asked.

'I'm Carol, I'm one of the carollers' she acknowledged the rest of the group.

'And what do you have to say about Trae?'

'Well, we were at the hospital carolling in August, as we do every year, and cheering people up, when Santa showed up, as he normally did. Then we heard Trae had killed Santa, and that we can't celebrate Christmas anymore, so now we are practising to celebrate Christmaslessness.'

'So it is because of Trae that we no longer have Christmas.'

'That's right, now we have to rewrite the songs, so instead of singing about Christmas, we sing about Christmaslessness.'

'Thank you, Carol. I'll let you all get back to your practise. You heard it here' George said to the camera 'Trae killed Christmas, he's been homeless, and he's interfered with job prospects of one of our inhabitants. I'm going to go see if I can find anyone else to interview, but for now, back to you in the studio.'

'Thank you, George. We'll come back later with updates as they come to hand-'

Octavius stood up and turned the television off. 'Oh, he won't do anything crazy, will he, Aaronn. He'll be fine, you said. Well, that doesn't look fine to me, and even worse, Trae's buddies survived, how did I miss noticing that?'

'I am not happy about this' Aaronn looked at them all 'we'll have to do something about this.'

'Already on it' Octavius ran out of the office.

'Where's he going?' Sloane looked at General Melon and Aaronn.

'I don't know, but it can only end in chaos. Let's go' Aaronn picked up his car keys and walked out with Sloane and General Melon following behind him. 'Oh great, Octavius has taken my car.'

'Now what?' Sloane asked, 'mine's in the shop.'

'And I jogged here' general Melon added.

'That leaves Trae's car, a hot pink convertible' Aaronn shook his head as he stared at the pink convertible. He walked over and felt on top of the front tyre. *Yep, typical, but thanks for leaving the keys.*

'So, where do we go?' Sloane asked when they were all in the car. *I hate pink.*

'If you were Octavius, where would you go if your enemy was at sea?' asked Aaronn.

'Get a boat and follow him' Sloane suggested tentatively.

'No, that's too placid.' General Melon observed 'Head to the fortress. He'll send out the scud missiles.'

'So, who's in favour of just sitting here, and listening to the car radio?' Sloane looked around and saw the others raise their hands. She turned the radio on, and a spark flew out.

'Well, we would listen to the radio' Aaronn started the car 'but you just broke it.' Aaronn reversed the car and headed out of the car park. As he went to put on the brakes to slow down so that he could enter the main road, he found himself hitting the floor with the pedal. 'Oh great, no brakes.'

General Melon yelled from the back seat 'Yippee, this will be a fun ride!'

'This isn't funny, sir, I can't stop the car.'

'I know, Aaronn, you'll have to crash it.'

'Joy.' Sloane put her seat belt on.

Octavius entered the fortress; an underground missile launch facility that sat near the wharf, not that anyone passing by would know that was what the building was for. To the normal passer-by it was a balloon factory. He switched on the radar system, and it crackled into life. A beeping noise soon emitted, as an object appeared on the screen.

He looked at the radar system. 'There you are, Trae, what are you up to?' He watched the green blip on the screen moving west. He punched in the co-ordinates of Trae's position into the nearby computer.

A few seconds later, a list of what was in the area was displayed on the screen. There was only one. Octavius looked at the computer and then at the radar. 'Why would you be heading to an oil rig?'

Octavius whistled – how Octavius can whistle with a beak is another mystery – as he pressed the buttons preparing the launch missile. He knew what he had to do.

Trae steered the battleship towards the unmanned oil rig. *Soon he'd get his revenge on Octavius.* As the boat headed towards the rig, Trae looked through his binoculars. *What are those little boats doing there?*

Oh, it's those hippies. Isn't that cute, they're protesting against the oil rig being here.

Trae read the signs through his binoculars. 'Oil is bad for marine life.' 'Protect our oceans – no more drilling.' He steered the battleship through the small boats and pulled up close to the oil rig. 'Hey!' one of the protesters yelled 'What do you think you're doing?'

'Anchors away!' Trae yelled and released the anchor which shot down towards the ocean but landed in one of the protesters boats.

'Man overboard!' the protester yelled as his boat sunk under the weight of the anchor which continued down to the seabed.

The water nearby surged as an explosion ripped through the water, causing the other boats to capsize. Trae realised his time was short if he was to act. He jumped from the battleship onto the oil rig with a backpack. He made his way to the central drilling shaft, and placed dynamite around it. Another explosion nearby confirmed his suspicions someone was trying to stop him. If he had to guess, his guess would be – Octavius.

Well, he's too late. He can't stop me. Trae set the timer and made his way back to the ship. He saw the bodies of the protesters floating nearby. *That last explosion must have killed them. Oh well.* He looked at his watch *thirty minutes, and boom.*

Trae started to move the ship back towards the island. *It's the only way to kill his kind.* Every now and then an explosion of water rose up as a missile hit the water. Trae checked his watch. He picked up the binoculars, went on deck, and looked at the oil rig. *And five, four, three, two, one* *Boom* there was an explosion on the oil rig.

The unmistakable black oil shot up into the air, and into the ocean. *Yes, I did it.* He went back to the cabin and steered towards the island. *Now, for the other oil rig on the other, side of the island.*

'Brace yourselves!' Aaronn yelled as they neared the fortress. He down shifted the gears which helped slow it down a fraction.

'I didn't know we had a balloon factory!' General Melon read the sign on the gate they flew passed.

'We don't. It's just so no one realises its true purpose.' Aaronn zoomed down passed the side of the building. He swerved the car around the back of the building and ploughed through the roller doors and crashed into the wall inside. Surprised that no one was seriously hurt, they stumbled from the car. They ran down the stairs to the room below.

'Octavius!' Aaronn yelled as he leapt out of the car 'don't you dare let off another missile!'

'Too late' Octavius pressed the button and launched the missile. He watched the progress of the missile. 'Yes, I got it.'

'What have you done?' Aaronn and the others half walked; half ran over to Octavius.

'I hit his ship' Octavius said gleefully.

Aaronn groaned as General Melon took charge. 'By my calculations' General Melon borrowed Sloane's notebook and wrote on a piece of paper. 'Yep, anything left from that explosion should wash up on the beach in the next few hours.'

General Melon's mobile rang. 'Hello, uh huh, just hold the line.' He handed the phone to Aaronn 'It's for you.'

'Hello, this is Aar-' Aaronn held the phone away from his ear as the person on the other end shouted.

'Gee, that guy sounded a little angry' Sloane remarked as Aaronn hung up and handed the phone back to General Melon.'

'Well, he should be. That was the head of the environment action group. They sent a plane out to check on their oil rig, but the oil rig apparently was blown up, there is oil everywhere. He wants to know who's paying to stop the flow, and the clean-up. Oh, and apparently the plane spotted someone floating on the wreckage.'

'It has to be that traitor' Octavius started to walk out the facility. 'C'mon he'll wash ashore soon enough, let's meet him, and see what he has to say for himself.'

*** XV ***

General Melon was taking Octavius, Aaronn and Sloane through some running exercises through the sand as they waited for Trae, and any other wreckage to come to shore. 'Alright let's run on the spot.' General Melon started jogging up and down on the spot. The others groaned.

'Hey guys' Sloane huffed 'anyone want to have a bet as to when Trae will wash up?'

'Not now, Sloane' General Melon said 'C'mon do some star jumps. Don't you want to live long and healthy like me?'

'No, what I really want, sir, is a really big chocolate milkshake, right now.'

'You'll never get into shape with that attitude, now come along, star jumps, everyone. And one, and two, and-'

'Guys, look' Sloane pointed to down the beach. *I've never been glad to see anyone in my life.* 'Sorry, general' she held her side from the pain as a stitch surged through 'But, I bet that's Trae.' She started to walk towards the dark lump lying in the shallows of the water, surrounded by an oily slick that seemed to go further than the eye could see.

'It is Trae, either that or a rock' Aaronn sprinted towards the body and lifted him up, then dropped him. 'Yuck, my uniform.'

'You can clean that at your own expense' General Melon said as he jogged up to them and continued jogging on the spot.

'You can pay for this, Trae' Aaronn told him as he helped Trae stand up. He let go of Trae and looked at his shirt that had oil on it now. He screwed his nose up 'You've made this stink, and you definitely stink, Trae.'

'Yeah, Trae' Sloane waved her hand in the air as though she was trying to get rid of the smell 'you reek.'

Exhausted Trae sank to his knees, lifted his head, and looked at the others. 'You' he stared at Octavius with a murderous look 'you sank my battleship.'

'Well, of course I did you Ecoterrorist. I can't believe you blew up that oil rig.'

'It was the only way to get rid of you and your kind.'

'See, Aaronn, he's picking on me.'

'Trae!' Pain's voice yell made them turn and look. Pain jogged up to the group 'Tell me Trae, what's it like to breathe that oil in. Could you feel your insides wanting to burst? Did the taste want to make you vomit?'

'You have got to be kidding' Trae choked.

They watched Pain run into the oil slickened water and submerge himself. He surfaced 'Thank you, Trae, I could barely breathe under there, and the pain, I love it. You should all try this; it will strengthen your insides. I must try to drown myself in this.' He submerged himself back under the oil slick.

'Are you sure, I can't kill him, Aaronn' Octavius said, 'it would put all of us out of our misery of having to deal with him, and it's not like anyone will miss him. Besides he is asking for it.'

'No, Octavius, you can't kill him' Aaronn helped Trae stand up, Sloane stood on the other side of Trae, and helped him stand.

'I can't believe I'm back here' Trae spoke huskily his throat sore from the salt water, and oil 'One more oil rig, then I was going for the mainland.'

'Sorry, Trae' Octavius adjusted his fedora 'but once you're on the island, you're always on the island.'

'But, but-'

'Not now, Trae' Aaronn ordered 'let's get you home.' They started to walk up the beach to the car park.

'But, what about, Peter the motorcycle dude, he made it off.'

'He was a special case.' General Melon jogged backwards 'do you know what you need to freshen up? Some exercise.'

'Does this island ever make sense?'

'And still he talks' Octavius juggled the car keys 'indignity after indignity.'

'She' General Melon corrected Octavius, as he took the keys off him, turned around, and jogged off to the car. 'Catch me if you can!'

'Well, I'm not running' Sloane let go of her hold on Trae as he seemed to be able to walk by himself. 'Yuck, you can pay to have my uniform cleaned too.'

By the time they reached the car general Melon was doing push ups against its side. 'About time you lot got here.' General Melon looked at his watch. 'That took you lot fifteen minutes to get here. In you get. I'm driving.'

'But, sir' Aaronn implored 'my car, I can't let anyone else drive it for five years.'

'Why, are you on probation?'

'I don't want to talk about it, but let's just say it involved Octavius, Sloane, Trae's car, and -'

'Heh, heh, heh say no more' General Melon cut Aaronn off, and handed him the keys.

Aaronn drove out of the car park and headed back into town. 'Thank goodness, the office is only twenty minutes away, the car stinks already. We'll have to discuss later who is going to pay for the clean-up.'

'It should be that traitor' Octavius looked behind him at Trae sitting in the back seat.

'It was so easy' Trae mumbled to himself 'I just had to blow up the oil rigs.'

'See, Aaronn, Trae's still picking on me' Octavius started to play with the radio dial.

Aaronn slapped Octavius across the tentacle and turned the radio on. 'Will you lot wind the windows down, it stinks in here? Trae you'll have to pay for detailing the car too.'

'Ow' Octavius glared at Aaronn 'I can't believe you hit me. Indignity after indignity.'

'Stop the car! Trae yelled out as they were almost halfway back to the office.

'What, I'm not stopping here' Aaronn turned the radio up and slowed down to take the bend in the road.

Trae opened the passenger door, and jumped out, rolling as he hit the ground. Momentarily stunned he stood up and ran. Aaronn stopped the car, and they got out to follow him, but they couldn't see him.

'Where'd he go?' Sloane held her hand over her eyes as she scanned the area 'I can't believe he disappeared like that. I don't think I've ever seen Trae run.'

'He can't go far, not with the weight he's carrying' General Melon practiced doing his squats 'there's nothing here but the base where they keep the helicopters, not that they use them very often.'

'Well, it's not worth driving' Aaronn pointed to the building on the opposite side of the road, and about ten metres away heading towards the beach. 'C'mon' Aaronn started to run, with the others not far behind 'just follow the oil footprint tracks.'

They could hear the noise of the helicopter as it was warming up in preparation to taking off. As they ran into the facility, they saw it lifting off. 'We're too late' Sloane said.

'Maybe not' Aaronn said as they continued to run towards the helicopter, but as they neared it, they saw it heading up, and not stopping.

'Don't worry, Aaronn, I'll deal with this' Octavius ran to a nearby helicopter and sat in it. He put the headset on and started the engine. After a few minutes he lifted off and followed Trae.

'This can't end well' Aaronn looked at Sloane and General Melon 'besides there wasn't enough warm up time.'

'If Octavius is at the helm, things just work out one way or the other' General Melon laughed.

'You don't know that' Sloane looked at the two helicopters that were now up in the sky, and now facing each other.

'They're both loaded with weapons, Sloane' Aaronn looked upwards 'and we are talking about Trae and Octavius.'

'Oh, that's no good' she paused and took out her notebook 'so, anyone wanna bet on the outcome.'

'Trae's going down' General Melon did some lunges 'oh, and he can pay for the helicopter to be cleaned, it'll be filthy now he's been in it.'

'That's the easy bet, sir, but okay' Sloane wrote on her notepad.

Trae and Octavius faced each other, weapons locked, and loaded. Octavius flicked a switch to turn on the speaker system. 'Trae, you've gone too far this time.'

'Me, you've gone too far. It's all your fault.'

'Well, this is getting us nowhere.'

'You're right, Octavius, this isn't getting us anywhere. That's why I'm going to destroy this island.' Trae started to laugh 'I'm going to destroy you once and for all.'

'Trae, I think you need to rethink your strategy. If you look at it from my perspective, I'll only end up looking like a hero again, which is great news for me.'

Trae stopped laughing and stared at Octavius. *Damn it, he's right. Even if I do manage to kill him, people will see him as a martyr, and still be completely oblivious to the fact that he is an octopus, and a murderous one at that.* 'I'm not having you immortalised! You freak!'

'I'm not the freak; you're the one who ate the chef.'

I'm not going to give him the satisfaction of winning. I'll let him live ... for now. Trae began to drop the helicopter's height and prepared to land.

'Well, I'm surprised' Aaronn said to no one in particular 'no blood shed, and no damage.'

Octavius followed behind. Trae had nearly landed when Octavius let off a volley of shots at Trae's helicopter. Several hit the side causing Trae to panic and lose control; the helicopter leaned to one side, the rotor hitting the ground, the body splitting apart. *What happened?* Trae groaned as he pulled himself up and saw Octavius land his helicopter. *Octavius there was no other answer. He was responsible.*

Trae watched Octavius get out of his helicopter, brush his fedora down and put it on. He whistled as he walked over to Trae. 'You had me going there for a minute' he slapped Trae across the back 'I thought you were actually going to do it.'

The pain from Octavius slapping him across the back shot through his body. He bit his lip to stop the expletive from being said. 'C'mon' Octavius pointed to the car 'Look Aaronn's waiting.'

'Anything broken, Trae' Aaronn asked as Trae and Octavius met up with them at the car.

'No, I just hurt all over.' He looked at Octavius 'Why?!'

'Because I can' Octavius opened the car door besides, you threatened me. Aaronn, I want that written up, that-'

'Not a word from anyone' Aaronn ordered as he started the car up and headed back to the office.

'Sir' Georgia, the new receptionist greeted them as they entered the office.

'Not now' Aaronn ushered General Melon, Sloane, Octavius, and Trae towards his office.

'But sir, this is important.

Aaronn sighed. *Could this day get any worse?* 'You lot go ahead. What is it?'

Georgia handed him a newspaper. 'You have to read the article on the front page.'

Aaronn read the article as he walked to his office. He walked in and slapped the paper down on the table. There on the front page was a blown-up photo of the photo that Trae had taken on his first day, of Aaron fighting with Octavius throwing the private. 'How did this get out? Did you leak this, Octavius?'

'Yeah, but the traitor snapped it.'

'I'm not a traitor' Trae threw his hands up in the air 'Oh, I give up.'

'Octavius, that is the slyest form of blame shifting I've ever seen from you.'

'Yeah, but who are you gonna hate more, me or Trae?

'Quick, sir' Sloane nudged General Melon 'who does Aaronn hate more, Trae or Octavius?'

'I don't like either of you' Aaronn picked up the paper and looked at it. 'Everybody, out' he ordered, I'll see you tomorrow.' He watched them leave, then he picked up the paper and looked at the article again. He threw it back down on the on the table and turned to leave. 'The animal activists are going to have me for this one.' He picked it up again and finally threw it in the bin then walked out.

*** XVI ***

Seven years later four black horses fitted with black plumes pulled a wooden wagon that was painted black behind them. The horses were led by a priest through the streets of the island heading towards the cemetery, which lay opposite Quicksand Valley.

On the wagon, lay a gold coffin, befitting of someone wealthy, or regal. On the lid of the coffin lay a simple wreath of seaweed, with a donut in the middle, and at the head of the coffin lid was engraved an epitaph in red letters 'Indignity after indignity.'

Gone were the days of the adoring crowds, that fed his ego as they cheered him every chance they got. Now just a small group of people waited by the pit for the arrival of the coffin.

"Admiral' Aaronn saluted Melon 'it's been a long time.'

'Yes, it has, general' Admiral Melon saluted Aaronn 'I can't believe I outlived him.'

'Well, I for one, am going to miss his crazy antics' Sloane wiped her hands on her jeans 'there'll never be anyone like Octavius.'

'Ain't that the truth. How's the auto repair shop, Sloane' Aaronn asked as they watched a wheelchair push a wheelchair behind the horse drawn hearse towards them.

'Oh, you know, business is up and down. More down than up I have to admit.' Sloane sighed 'I just don't understand why everything I touch blows up or gets a life of its own. Maybe it's like some sort of gift in reverse, that I was just born with this talent.'

'Is that Trae?' Admiral Melon squinted as the nurse overtook the horses as they plodded slowly along. The sun was shining and creating a glare, but even though he wasn't sure, he as well as the others knew who it was, that was being pushed in the wheelchair, as they had been expecting him to attend the funeral. And he was the only one who hadn't arrived until now.

They watched as the nurse overtook the horses, and began to push the chair forward, and let go, then walk up to it, and push it again, then let go as soon as she pushed it, and then walked up to it.

She turned from the road, for the last leg to where the group stood, and gave the chair a little push, but didn't seem to realise, or maybe she did, that the final stretch to where the others were waiting was a slight downhill slope. She pushed the chair, and it started to roll towards the group, she ran behind it trying to catch up to it, while Trae screamed as he waved his hands around.

Admiral Melon grabbed hold of the chair as it was rolling by. As he grabbed it, the momentum made it, and Admiral Melon spin around a couple of times in a circle. 'Wheeeeee' the admiral said, 'wasn't that fun?'

'No, sir' Trae held his head in his hands 'I'm dizzy.'

'At least you were strapped in' Sloane took a photo with her camera.

'I am so sorry' the nurse said breathlessly as she caught up to the group.

'Is it true?' Trae asked still strapped to his chair 'They told me he was dead.'

'Yes, Trae' Sloane squatted next to him 'Octavius has died of old age.'

'I want to make sure. I have to be sure that he's dead.'

'Trae' Aaronn waved the nurse who had brought Trae away 'it's true. Octavius is dead.'

Admiral Melon untied Trae from the chair. 'I think you'll be fine now. The doctors told me your therapy sessions have been going quite well.'

'Thank you, sir' Trae stretched his arms over his head, and stood up slowly head, his hair now oily and long, hung down to his waist, a beard that he had grown he had parted in the middle and tied with orange bands, and his clothes were loose fitting. 'I still can't believe you built an asylum in Quicksand Valley.'

'It was Octavius's idea' Admiral Melon laughed 'and it was named after you. Saint Trae Asylum. Did you like the angel that Octavius put up over the door? It looked so much like you.'

'But sir, you forgot about me until last year. I had to scavenged for food, and the building was sinking. I had no one to talk to except a mouse who stole my crumb of bread, and for a family of cockroaches, and even they turned their back on me. I had to survive eating scorpions.'

'Well, if it wasn't for Octavius reminding us, you'd be under by now. But look on the bright side. Look at all the weight you've lost, but you will need to get rid of that beard and get yourself a haircut' Admiral Melon looked at Trae's beard, which was as long as his hair. 'That is not a regulation hair style. I know the island has few rules, and we usually let a few things go by unnoticed, but we do require neatness.'

'Whatever, I'll get it cut later. You're not listening to me. Octavius tormented me in the new building.'

'He missed you, Trae' Admiral Melon said, 'but all that is behind us, the poor little squidling is dead.'

'He's not a squidling' Trae stomped his foot up and down 'he's an octopus! Well, a dead octopus, but still, he's an octopus.'

'Shush, give the guy some respect, he's done a lot for this island' Sloane said.

The horses plodded their way towards the group, led by the priest. As the horses stopped, the priest sprinkled some water on the coffin and said a quiet prayer. Aaronn, Sloane, Melon, and the priest lifted the coffin off. 'He's heavier than I thought' Sloane voiced her thoughts out loud. They put the coffin on the ground next to the hole.

Before anyone could stop him, Trae jumped on top of the coffin and started to dance. 'Yes, he's dead, he's finally dead, it's over, it's over!' Trae stopped dancing, jumped off ran, and hid behind Admiral Melon. 'Did you hear that?'

They all looked at each other confused except for Aaronn who was grinning. 'Trae, you haven't changed a bit. What did you think you heard?'

'He spoke. I heard him. He said, indignity after indignity like he always does.'

Melon pushed Trae away from him 'That sounds like the little squirt I knew. But, Trae, if you heard his ghost, then that means you'll have to spend eternity with him in the afterlife.'

As the coffin was lowered, and the priest was praying, Trae pondered the admiral's words. *An eternity with Octavius! That meant like forever!* He shook his fist at the sky … *Why?* Trae dropped on the ground and cried out 'Why?' before he pounded the ground with his fists 'Why? Why? Why?'

'See, he does miss Octavius' Sloane said to Aaronn 'and you said he wouldn't. You owe me ten dollars.'

The group stood around the grave, each with their own thoughts of Octavius as the coffin was lowered into the grave, and the grave diggers began to fill in the hole. 'So, let's go get a coffee, and doughnuts, in remembrance' Aaronn suggested after a few shovel loads of dirt had been thrown in.

Trae lingered at the grave site as they headed off. Sloane stopped, and turned 'Trae, are you coming?'

'But don't I have to go back to the asylum?' Trae walked towards them.

'No' Admiral Melon slapped him on the back. 'You're free to go, besides the asylum is no longer able to be seen, and you don't have to go back to the hospital either.'

'Free' Trae started to walk with the group to Aaronn's car. 'I don't have to go back!'

'No, we figure you'll always be the way you are' Aaronn confirmed 'besides, we figure that with Octavius gone, you'll be much better.' Aaronn started the car when they had all settled in and headed off to Octavius's favourite doughnut shop.

*** XVII ***

'Trae, it's been three years, since he died' Aaronn stated. 'Three very long years. Will you give it up, and just accept Octavius is dead? We all feel his loss, Trae. Life isn't the same without him, but he is dead and buried.'

'But the phone calls, Aaronn, I hear the jangling of chains, and the whispering outside my window at night. I know it's Octavius. How else did those red lollies get in my shower head?'

'I have to admit that was funny?'

'I thought there was blood coming out of it and my hair was all sticky!' Trae fumed 'And what about this morning when I had my shower, and found the word "Murderer" written on the mirror, what about that?'

'Obviously it's just someone playing tricks on you.'

'And that person is Octavius, I'm telling you.'

'Enough, Trae. Just go home, and get some rest, it's late.'

'But Aaronn!'

Aaronn looked up from his paperwork. 'Trae, I am still dealing with the oil company's demands from your last stunt. I said go home. Now, go!'

'Morning, Aaronn' Sloane walked in with her coffee 'I'm here for my week's training. I have to admit, it's a bit boring without Octavius around.'

'You sick of your workshop.'

'I love tinkering around, even if I don't get much business. People think I'm jinxed or something.'

'Well, if you listen to Trae, he thinks Octavius is still alive.'

'Poor, Trae' Sloane looked around 'he's so lost without Octavius. Where is he?'

'I don't know, but it's not like him to be late.'

Sloane pulled her phone out and pressed Trae's number.

'He won't answer, I've tried.'

'Do you want me to check on him?' Sloane put her phone back in her pocket.

'You can come with me' Aaronn said 'I'll leave Pain in charge here. He'll love to take the soldiers for a run.'

'I'm surprised he's still here, I thought he'd have left the island.'

'You know the rules, Sloane' Aaronn unlocked the car 'once you're on the island you can't leave.'

'Well, his car is still here' Sloane noted as Aaron pulled into the driveway, and parked.

'This is Trae, we're talking about' Aaronn said as they got out and walked up to the front door. 'Of course, he's here. He doesn't go anywhere without driving, even if it's to the corner of the street, he'll drive. I must talk to him about his laziness.' He knocked, but there was no answer.

'Allow me' Sloane said as she lifted the fern that sat near the front door. 'Yep' she picked up a key' he's so easy to read, she unlocked the door.

They walked in and looked around. 'Everything seems to be in order' she said.

They walked through the house and checked every room. 'Well, the only room left is this one' Aaronn tried the door 'but it doesn't open.'

Sloane gave the door a shove 'No, it's stuck, not locked. Help me.'

Together they pushed their weight against the door. The door gave enough for Sloane to reach in, and flick the light switch on. She looked at the floor 'building blocks?'

Aaronn shoved the door so that it opened enough for them to squeeze in. The floor was covered in building blocks. In the middle lay a rake, with Trae lying unconscious amongst them all. They walked to the middle of the floor, and shifted the building blocks out of the way with their feet as they went. As they lifted Trae up, he groaned, and came to.

'That's it, Trae' Aaronn said, 'time to wake up.' They helped him out of the room, and led him to the lounge room, where they laid him on the couch. 'What happened?'

Trae groaned 'I don't know. I went to bed, I heard the doorbell, got up to answer it, but when I stepped on the floor, I trod on something sharp, and then I had something hit me in the head, the next thing I know was you two standing over me.'

'C'mon, let's get you checked out' They helped Trae stand up, and helped him out to the car.

'I'm telling you it's Octavius.'

'He's dead, Trae, but obviously someone is annoying you' Sloane said, 'I'll check it out once you're out of the hospital.'

Trae yawned as he stirred in his bed. *I feel so much better. That sleeping pill the hospital really zonked me out. Maybe they're right. I just need a few nights of decent sleep.* He looked at his bedside clock and scratched his head. *0400, I'm so glad I didn't have to stay the night in hospital.* He got up and pulled a pair of orange boxers on.

He sniffed the coffee he made. *Mmm nothing beats the smell of coffee first thing, oh, and reading the paper.* He opened the front door to get the paper. *What is that smell?* He sniffed the air again. *That … that's petrol!* He grabbed the torch which lay on a table next to the door and walked outside.

The smell of fuel was so intense, his head began to hurt. Trae swung the light from the torch across the grass, trying to find where it came from. He saw a fuel can lying on the grass with a length of hose sticking out of it. *What the?* He shone the light on the hose and followed it, along the grass up into the petrol tank of his car.

As he walked closer to his car, he saw that his car had its wheels removed, and was now sitting up on bricks. *Octavius. I know it's him.* He threw the torch on the ground in disgust and walked off towards Aaronn's house.

'Hey, we have a dress code' a passing motorist yelled.

I don't care. Stupid octopus. I know it's him. No one else would torment me like he does. He's not dead, I just have to prove it.

He yawned as he walked up the driveway to Aaronn's door and pounded on it. 'What?' Aaronn grumbled as he opened the door a few minutes later. He sipped the coffee that he was holding 'Trae, do you have any idea of the time. And why can't you put a dressing gown on like I do, especially if you're just going to wear those orange boxers? They're a bit bright for this hour of the morning.'

'Aaronn' Trae tried to keep calm 'someone has siphoned the fuel out of my car and removed the wheels.'

'You could've waited until later, and reported that to the pol-'

'I couldn't wait. I know it's Octavius.'

'Trae, Octavius is dead.'

'No, he's not. I know he's not dead. I know it, I know his style. This just smells of Octavius's handiwork. Why can't you see that?'

'Snap out of it, Trae' Aaronn ordered 'He's dead. Someone is just annoying you.'

'But!'

'No buts. C'mon I'll give you a lift home.' Aaronn took his dressing gown off.

'You wear your uniform to bed?'

'Of course,' Aaronn pulled his car keys from his pocket, and shut the front door 'one should be ready for any situation that may come up.' He looked at Trae. 'You should remember that.' He grabbed a t-shirt from the back seat of the car and handed it to Trae. 'Put that on' he started the car and drove Trae back home.

'I'll even wait until you get inside' Aaronn said as he pulled into driveway and parked behind Trae's car. While Trae walked to his door, Aaronn typed a message on his phone to Sloane 'I really need to find out who's annoying-'

'AARONN!' Trae's scream cut through his thoughts as he was texting.

What now? He got out of his car and walked to the front door. 'Wow, would you look at that.'

'Now do you believe me. Look!' Trae stared at the doorway that was now bricked up 'Who else would do something like this, but Octavius.' Trae kicked the doorway 'Ow, that hurt.'

'Trae, that's not how you do it' Dr Pain said behind them.

'What are you doing here, Pain?' Aaronn asked.

'I was going for a run, and I saw Trae not injuring himself properly.'

'No, he was showing me someone had bricked up his doorway.'

'But it's a perfect opportunity to do some head strengthening exercises. I'll show you.' Dr Pain picked Trae up and held him as though he were a battering ram. 'Stop wriggling, this is for your own good.' Dr Pain took several steps backwards and prepared to run towards the bricks.

'AARONN!'

'Stop!' Aaronn ordered as he stood in front of the brick doorway 'Put Trae down!'

'But!'

'Down!'

'Alright, but can I hit the wall. Nothing builds character like pain.'

Aaronn shook his head and stepped out of the way. They watched as Dr Pain ran as fast as he could and slammed his head into the bricks. He staggered backwards and shook his head. 'Oh, that feels good' he said as he lined up for another run.

'C'mon Trae let's go to the office. There'll be a change of clothes there, and maybe some peace.'

'Can I drive?' Trae asked.

'Sure' Aaronn tossed the keys to him 'I can't see why not. It's not like Octavius is around to cause trouble.'

As they drove towards the office, Trae retold Aaronn all the things that had been happening. Aaronn nodded as he had heard it all before. Trae thumped the steering wheel and said, 'I'm telling you; Octavius is still alive, why won't you believe me?'

'And I'm tellin-' Aaronn's sentence was cut short, as he automatically put his hands up on the dashboard, because Trae slammed the brakes on. The cars behind couldn't stop in time, and banged into the rear of Aaronn's car, shunting it onto the footpath, and into a tree.

'My car!' Aaronn got out to look at the damage.

'Stuff your car' Trae grabbed his arm 'look over there!' Aaronn looked at where Trae was pointing. 'I told you' Trae started to drag Aaronn towards the park, where Octavius was raking up leaves into a pile.

'Octavius?' Aaronn said incredulously.

Octavius stopped raking the leaves up and looked at them. 'You're supposed to be dead!' Trae said.

'In your dreams, Traitor' Octavius said. 'I can't believe you buried me. I was just sleeping.'

'Sorry, Octavius, but you didn't wake up, so we figured you know, you were dead' Aaronn explained 'but how did you get out?'

'It took hours upon hours of me clawing my way through the wood and dirt, and I had no water to keep my skin clean and wet. Look at my tentacles they have blisters.'

'You can't have blisters' Trae said, 'you're an octopus.'

'If you're such an expert, how come you didn't know that I was just sleeping?'

'Because you had me locked up in an asylum!'

'Oh, yeah' Octavius looked at Trae 'I see they let you out.' He looked Trae up and down and laughed 'You do know, you forgot to wear pants today.'

'Okay you two' Aaronn looked at the tow truck that had arrived to remove his car 'let's continue this at the office. At least it's a nice day for a walk, and it's not too far away.'

'Sure, but let's stop for coffee and a few donuts first' Octavius started to walk ahead of the others 'I can't wait to see Sloane. She's going to be so surprised to see me.'

*** XVIII ***

Oh, what now? Trae went to answer his door. 'What do you want? And stop ringing the doorbell' he smacked Octavius's tentacle away from the doorbell.

'Ow, is that any way to treat someone who's bought you a gift?' Octavius walked in, and held out with one of his tentacles, a small box that had a piece of frayed string tied around it.

'You bought me a present?' Trae accepted the present that Octavius handed him 'that's so thoughtful. I never expected that from you, what's the occasion?'

'Happy Christmaslessness' Octavius sat on the sofa and started to flick through the channels. 'How could I not get the person who destroyed Christmas a present? You deserve this.'

Trae looked at the date on his mobile. 'Oh my gosh it's nearly Christmas. I can't believe how fast the year has gone.' He unwrapped the present and opened the box 'There's nothing in here.'

'Of course not. There's no more Christmas, remember, thanks to you.'

'It wasn't my fault, you're the one who killed Santa.'

'But you're the one everyone blamed' Octavius flicked through the channels 'and that's what matters. Hey check this out.'

Trae looked at the TV screen 'That's Sloane, turn it up.' They watched the footage on the screen of Sloane being surrounded by angry citizens who were yelling at her as they waved pitchforks, and lit torches in her face. 'Oh she has really riled them up, I wonder what she did?'

'Shush!' Octavius went to slap Trae across the head, but he ducked 'this is the best program I've seen.'

'This is Sloane, and those people could do her some serious harm.'

'She's a witch!' someone yelled.

'Burn her at the stake!' yelled another person.

'You got popcorn? This is definitely way better than the movies' Octavius laughed. 'Sloane will be fine, don't worry about her. Oh, what? No, don't you dare. Oh, you are, aren't you, you spoilsport!' he yelled at the TV as Aaronn pushed his way through the crowd.

'She's not a witch' Aaronn could be heard on the TV 'she's just incompetent.'

'She's a witch, burn her!' they yelled 'Burn her, burn her!' They chanted and waved their pitchforks towards her as they yelled.

Aaronn tried to reason with them, but the crowd got louder, and more threatening. He pulled an object out of his pocket threw it on the ground, and smoke emerged. Octavius changed channel 'Well that's that, Aaronn has helped her escape. Now we won't see them burn her.'

'Octavius! What if Sloane died?'

'What? No that wouldn't have happened, they said she was a witch, so even fire would've run away from her. Just look at what happens when she touches machinery.' Octavius sighed 'It was a good show until Aaronn showed up.'

Bang Bang Bang

Oh, what now? Trae went to answer the door 'Stop pounding-' His words were cut off as Sloane and Aaronn pushed their way in and shut the door behind them.

'That was close' Aaronn said.

'And why are you two here?' Trae sighed as he watched them sit next to Octavius, and fight for the remote.

'Your place was close by. Those people are nuts out there' Aaronn went to the fridge 'by the way, can we stay here tonight?'

'What?! No, why?!"

'It's just so the natives calm down. Sloane here really riled them up.'

'It wasn't my fault' Sloane said 'all I did was walk past a few cars, and their alarms went off by themselves. And maybe, a couple of letterboxes kind of got a life of their own, and started fighting in the middle of the street, and it went downhill from there.'

'Let us stay, Trae' Octavius said, 'it'll be great, just like a sleep over.'

'You won't even know that we've been here' Aaronn added.

Trae groaned 'There's some blankets in the cupboard, I am going to sleep, I don't want any of you here by the time I wake up.'

What's that noise? Trae coughed as he opened his eyes. *Smoke alarm. Fire, there's a fire.* He coughed as he dropped to the ground and crawled to the front door. *Must get out* he fumbled with the door handle, before finally opening it, and dragging himself out. He gasped, and choked as he breathed the fresh air.

'Here' Aaronn put Trae's arm around his shoulder and helped him to walk to the front kerb where a crowd of people had gathered to watch.

'YOU!' Trae looked at Octavius, who was busy sweeping embers and ash into the neighbour's yard and ignoring the neighbour swearing at him. 'You did this, didn't you?'

'Well, yes, but I had a good reason' Octavius followed them onto the kerb.

'What possible reason could you have to set fire to my house?' Trae looked around 'And where the hell is the fire brigade?'

'Trae, I saw a spider?'

Trae stared at Octavius, as the siren of the fire brigade finally could be heard. 'What took you so long?' he asked one of the firefighters as they got out of the truck.

'Sorry, but someone sent us to the other side of the island. False alarm' he shrugged and helped the others unroll the hose and start extinguishing the fire.

Trae took a deep breath before looking at Octavius, and speaking through clenched teeth he said, 'And you couldn't use a shoe like any normal person would?'

'It was a big spider. Sometimes fire is the only way to get rid of them' Octavius reasoned.

'Aaronn!' Trae stared at Octavius with a murderous look, his fists clenched by his side.

'Calm down, Trae, you should know by now that Octavius can sometimes go a little overboard.'

'A little overboard. He set my house on fire.'

'I've organised a replacement' Aaronn said, as he thanked the firefighters for the job they did.

'Oh' Octavius said, 'you mean Trae's not going to be homeless.'

'No, Sloane is going to take him there now.'

'Drats, I was hoping for a twofer.'

'What is a twofer?' Trae asked as Sloane pulled up in a car.

'Two for one' Octavius said, 'I killed the spider, but I thought I'd get the bonus of seeing you homeless again.'

'NO!' Aaronn grabbed Trae, as he went to strangle Octavius. Aaronn forced him into the car 'Go Sloane, and don't stop till you drop him off' he slammed the door shut, then turned to face Octavius.

'I know' Octavius tried to look guilty 'I did a bad thing.'

'Well, what's done is done, let's call it a night.'

'Do you think, Trae will still be mad in the morning?' Octavius said as he got into his car.

'That is one thing I can guarantee' Aaronn walked off to talk to the fire chief before heading home.

XIX

Trae yawned and stretched *What a day?* He stood up and went to walk out of his office when he saw people running past the doorway. 'Hey what's going on?' he grabbed someone's arm to stop them running.

'Let me go, he's here!' the man pulled away from Trae and ran off down the corridor.

'People!' Octavius's voice came over the loudspeaker 'Don't panic. I have it all under control!'

Trae watched as instantly people stopped panicking and started to walk normally. *Wow! Octavius speaks and everyone listens. Why does that still surprise me?*

'Quick, Trae' Sloane said, 'what's your bet?'

'Bet? What are we betting on?' Trae walked with Sloane through the building towards the front door.

'Aaronn' Sloane stopped at his office door 'what's your bet?'

'What are you betting on?' Trae asked.

'Well,' Aaronn swallowed his coffee 'Santa's reindeer have turned up-'

'Oh wow, his reindeer' Trae paused 'but how?'

'One of Santa's elves is trying to do Santa's round' Aaronn said.

'But I put a stop to that' Octavius said from behind them 'we just have a little problem now.

'What problem could there be?' Trae asked 'Santa's reindeer are so nice. Take Dasher and Dancer-'

'Oh, Trae' Octavius put a tentacle around Trae's shoulders 'Trae, Trae, Trae, poor gullible Trae. They're not the names of Santa's reindeer.'

'What? They're not, what are their names?'

'You don't want to know' Aaronn started to say but Octavius cut in and started to sing.

'There was Pincher, and Panzer, Cancer and Flasher, Stupid and Vomit, Blazen and Stoner, but the most famous one of all is Rude Dolphin' Octavius cackled. 'And now that Santa is dead, and the elf is dead, the magic has worn off, and they have gone rogue, so they have to die too' he laughed and ran off.

'He gave Pain a head start' Sloane said, 'What's the bet Aaronn?'

'I am going to go ... they get four each, I don't think either will get Rude Dolphin.'

'Trae?'

'You people are nuts. I think I'm going to be sick.'

'You're no fun' Sloane said, 'I think Octavius will get the most.'

'After tonight' Aaronn decided, 'I think we need to look at your gambling problem.'

'Problem, I don't have a problem' Sloane said as she went into someone's office 'hey what odds do you want on how many reindeer Octavius kills.'

'She has a problem' Trae said as he and Aaronn walked out of the office doors. 'Oh wow, check it out' The night was lit up with flashing lights of red and green. Trae started to move his body in a jerkily manner.

'What are you doing?'

'I'm dancing.'

'While the neighbourhood is ablaze? You're despicable and depraved! Octavius who had returned to get something, criticised as he left again. And indeed, the neighbourhood was being torched by none other than one of Santa's reindeer.

'Well stop it, that's disturbing. Anyway, that fire breathing reindeer is Blazen' Aaronn said just as a shot echoed and the light show stopped. 'Correction, that was Blazen.'

'Gotcha Blazen' Octavius said as he pushed his fedora back slightly. He looked around. 'Aha' he saw the sled with a reindeer still standing there, a glazed look in its eyes, and drool coming from its mouth. 'You must be Stupid. Thanks for making it easy for me' he said as he shot the reindeer and walked off.

As Octavius was passing by a tree, a reindeer, wearing a raincoat stepped out from behind it, and stood in front of him. 'Hey bud' the reindeer opened one side of the coat it was wearing 'wanna watch?'

'I like that gold watch, Pincher' Octavius said as he raised his gun 'but I'm more of a lead man.'

'Hold on, what's say we make a deal. I'm sure I've got something you'd like' Pincher opened the other side of his coat 'look. I've got diamond necklaces, rings, knives. What about a knife? You look like a knife man of impeccable tastes.'

'Nope, I'm definitely a gun type of octopus' he pulled the trigger 'Three down, six more to go.'

'Octavius' Dr Pain ran past him 'stop taking my kills.'

'You're just slow' Octavius laughed 'there's still six more, but they have to be killed tonight. If they're not killed by midnight, they'll return to the North Pole until next year, and I'm not letting that happen, so try and beat me.' He laughed as he ran off. He looked back and saw Pain shaking his fist at him.

'Alright' Octavius slowed to a walk passed the swimming pool, pulled a pen and a piece of paper out of his fedora, and crossed out the names of the reindeer he had killed.

'Oh, I am so good looking, but I have got to work out my muscles some more.'

Octavius looked over to where he heard the voice coming from. *Ah, Panzer looks like you got distracted.* He looked at the reindeer that was lying on his front, his head resting on his paws, as he gazed into the swimming pool, admiring his reflection, his guns, and grenades that he had been using, lay next to him.

You guys make it easy for me. Octavius crept into the pool area, slid into the water, and swam underneath to where Panzer was still staring at his reflection. Reaching up with two of his tentacles, Octavius pulled Panzer under, and drowned him, then got out, and walked off to find his next kill.

As he walked through the streets, he saw a cloud of smoke. The closer he got, the more he started to cough. He peered through the smoke, and saw Pain and Cancer smoking, whilst holding another two cigarettes that had been lit. 'Hey Cancer, don't you know smoking is bad for you' he took aim and fired.

'Hey' Pain looked at the corpse next to him, before turning and seeing Octavius. 'You.'

'Yep, and that's another kill to me, and zero to you' Octavius walked off laughing. Music boomed out from the nightclub, as he walked by. He started to move in time with the music, when he saw Stoner leaning up against the door frame, smoking a joint. 'Want one?'

Stoner asked Octavius as he took another puff 'this is so good.'

Octavius danced over to where Stoner was and looked him over. 'You are so wasted' Stoner started to laugh and look around as though he were watching something that wasn't there. Octavius shook his head and shot Stoner before he went into the nightclub to see if there were any others.

As he danced to the music, he let of a volley of shots, and the patrons all cheered. They bought Octavius a drink and the locals toasted him, and his success. Octavius drank the beer, and then went to the men's toilets before heading back out. He pushed the door open and heard a strange choking sound 'That doesn't sound healthy' he said to himself and pushed the doors of the cubical open. There was Vomit who was kneeling at the toilet vomiting.

'I feel so ill' Vomit looked at Octavius.

'I'll put you out of your misery' misery' he shot Vomit, 'Yuck, look at the mess you've made, and you've stunk up the place' he flushed the toilet. 'At least that's a little better.'

He walked out of the nightclub and heard people yelling 'Stop!' and the men putting their hands across their partners eyes, so they didn't see Flasher as he opened and shut his raincoat yelling 'Check it out!'

'Don't worry everyone' Octavius shot Flasher 'I've fixed the problem.' Everyone cheered as Flasher lay dead on the road.

A car with a trailer pulled up and stopped near Flasher and Octavius. Sloane got out 'Good job, brigadier, you got them all except for Rude Dolphin.'

'Yeah, he's a tricky one, that one.'

Pain came running up to Sloane and Octavius. 'Octavius, you are greater than me. and before midnight too.'

'Why before midnight?' Sloane asked confused.'

Because they would've disappeared back to the North Pole' Pain told her.

'Octavius? I might have stretched the truth a little, and said that, but I really wanted to kill them all tonight.'

'Will you shoot me too' Pain knelt in front of Octavius.

'Well, seeing as you asked so nice-.'

'No, Brigadier' Sloane intervened.

'But, Sloane' Octavius reasoned 'it's natural selection. C'mon let me put the island out of its misery.'

'NO!' Sloane jerked her head around 'everyone duck!'

Rude Dolphin flew overhead and shot laser beams out of his eyes towards them. 'I got him' Octavius yelled as he shot a volley of shots towards the reindeer. 'You wait' he yelled as the reindeer flew off 'I'll get you.'

'You've had a busy night, brigadier' Sloane said 'you should get some rest. Give me your guns, sir.'

'Oh, indignity after indignity' Octavius threw the guns at her. One dropped to the ground and discharged.

'Ow' Pain yelled as he limped off 'thank you, Octavius.'

'Ahh, my work is done here except for you Rude Dolphin' Octavius shook his tentacle at Rude Dolphin as he could still see him in the distance 'I'll get you yet.' Then he began to whistle as he wandered off leaving Sloane to dispose of the bodies.

XX

Aaronn hung up the phone as Octavius walked into his office the following morning. 'I thought you'd have slept in after the busy night you had last night.'

'Always up bright and early. That Rude Dolphin is a tricky one to get, I have to admit. Here' Octavius handed Aaronn a coffee 'I thought you might need this though.'

'Thanks, someone has just reported a hole of some kind has appeared in the footpath near the park. I'll have to assign some-'

'Ooh, ooh, me ... Pick me, pick me' Octavius jumped up and down 'you can trust me.'

'I guess you can't get into too much trouble. All you have to do is make sure it's not too deep, and rope it off so no one trips in it, I'll get the repair crew out tomorrow to fix it.'

'I'll get right on it.'

'Take a couple of people with you.' Aaronn looked at Octavius 'Yes, I know you're awesome, and can do this on your own, but just in case ... you know, maybe to help keep people away.'

'Indignity after indignity. This is how you treat me, and after everything I've done. I get no respect' he folded two of his tentacles across his front 'fine. I'll take trumpet nose, and some other loser.' He stormed out of the office.

Octavius and the two soldiers stared at the hole. 'That's a big hole' Octavius shoved one of the soldiers into the hole. "It's a bit deeper than what Aaronn thinks, you check it out trumpet nose' he laughed as the soldier screamed as he fell.

'Hey, it's a cavern' the soldier popped his head back up 'there's some steps carved into the side, and you should check out the machine down here.'

'I got to see' Octavius yanked the soldier out of the hole and climbed down. 'C'mon' he ordered the soldiers to follow him.

A shaft of light filtered into the hole, showing what looked like a conveyor belt, that ran around the wall of the cavern. At the beginning was what looked like a computerised system, with a machine of some type attached.

'Well,' Octavius said 'there's only one thing to do.'

'Report this to Aaronn' one of the soldiers said as he pulled out his phone.

'Don't be stupid' Octavius slapped the phone out of his hand and walked over to the terminal 'it's time to press buttons and see what this baby does.'

'But, but sir!'

Octavius ignored the soldier and started to press the buttons on the console. 'Alright' he said as the machine started up 'now, what are you for?' He looked at the container shaped box at the beginning of the conveyor belt, as the belt started to move. 'This has to produce something' he said to himself 'I wonder?'

He took his fedora off, put it in the entrance of the container, and pressed what appeared to be a counter button, so that it read number one. The machine started to make a whirring noise, and Octavius's fedora moved into the container, and after a few minutes, it moved out along the conveyor belt, followed by a replica.

'Check it out' Octavius put his fedora on and held the duplicate 'it's a duplicator.'

'I don't think that we should mess with this, sir' one of the soldiers said, 'we should report this.'

'Yes, yes, after I ...' Octavius pressed the start button, and jumped inside the machine. Once through, he jumped off the conveyor belt. Within a couple of minutes, a duplicate of Octavius emerged. He watched it move along the conveyor belt, to the end where it jumped off. 'Alright, it's a cloning machine.'

He pushed the counter button up as high as it could go. 'There can never be enough of me' he said as he jumped into the machine once more. He leapt of the conveyor belt, when he had come through the duplicator, and laughed, as he watched copies of himself appear, and travel along the conveyor belt, till they got to the end where they fell on the floor and started to walk around.

'I don't like the sound of the machine' one of the soldiers said, 'or that smoke.'

The belt started to go faster, and the clones of Octavius kept coming; the cavern was fast filling up with clones. 'I'm out of here' one of the soldiers said.

'Not before me' they tussled with each other, as they clambered up the rungs to the top, and got out. 'Oh no!' they watched as the clones of Octavius began to climb out of the hole, with some standing in groups, while others walked off.

An explosion sounded from within the hole, and a cloud of smoke wafted out. 'This is not good' one of the soldiers pulled his mobile out, and dialled Aaronn's number. 'Typical, it's gone to voicemail. Aaronn it's not our fault, we couldn't stop him.'

Octavius climbed out 'We hit a little snag, the machine broke, but look at all the me's.'

He looked at the soldiers. 'What? What's the matter?'

'Well, sir' one of the soldiers said 'we don't know if you, are actually you. You all look the same, especially in this light' the soldier looked at his watch, and then at the sun that had begun to go down.'

'Indignity after indignity' Octavius paused 'well there's only one thing to do.' He walked to the car they had come in and opened the boot. He took out several guns 'I have to kill them. There is only one me.' The soldiers watched as Octavius set about killing the clones and knew that a long night lay ahead.

'AARONN!' Trae's voice echoed through the building.

'Problem?' Aaronn leaned up against the door.

Trae clenched his fists, and said through gritted teeth 'Why is my office filled with fedoras?'

'Well, if you answered your phone when we rang last night, you'd know that Octavius had an oopsy.'

'I was asleep, what happened?'

'Octavius managed to find a cloning machine, and cloned himself, but when he realised that no one would be able to tell which was the real Octavius, he started to kill them off. Unfortunately, we think some might have gotten off the island, we just don't know how many.'

'What makes you think that' Trae was finding it hard to keep his temper in check.

'Admiral Melon said that he saw a news report about two octopuses, wearing a fedora and scarf, duelling in the main street of a town in America with swords, and they were yelling "Indignity after indignity"' Aaronn laughed. 'But Octavius wanted to keep the fedoras as a memento, and sorry, but yours was the only free space.' Aaronn looked at Trae's expression 'Look, I told him I wasn't happy. I'll get someone to move them.'

'Don't bother, I'll do it myself' Trae stomped off to find garbage bags. *Stupid octopus.*

Trae was taking the last garbage bag filled with fedoras down to a nearby truck, when Octavius drove in. He threw the bag into the back, and walked over to Octavius who was getting out of the car.

'Hi Trae, hey!' Octavius complained as Trae grabbed his fedora and ran to the truck.

'If you want your hat' he yelled as he reversed the truck 'you'd better catch me before it gets tossed in with the rest.'

'You fiend' Octavius waved his tentacle at Trae who had driven off. He got back into his car, and followed Trae, honking his car horn, as he tried to get him to pull over. 'How does he steal vehicles so deftly?!' Octavius shook his tentacle as he followed Trae.

Trae drove through the gates of the rubbish dump, reversed the truck into the loading bay, and tipped the bags out onto the floor. He got out and started to empty the bags onto the conveyor belt that moved towards a furnace.

'Aarrgh, Trae, stop!' Octavius yelled as he looked at the line of fedoras that were moving and falling into the furnace.

'What's wrong, lost your hat. I wonder which one it is?' Trae continued to empty bags onto the belt. 'They're all the same, but you'd better try them on before they get burnt.'

"No, it's not that one. No, it's not that one. No, no, no, no' Octavius said as he stood near the furnace opening, picked up, tried a hat on, then threw it back on the belt 'you are so going to pay!'

'I paid a long time ago by coming to this island. Oh, maybe this is it' Trae held a fedora out to Octavius 'it would be a shame if this got burnt.'

'Don't you dare' Octavius walked towards him 'gimme my hat back!'

'Catch' Trae threw the hat up in the air, and towards Octavius. 'Ooops!' As Octavius went to catch it, his tentacle hit it, and sent it flying towards the furnace. 'Not my fault!' Trae ran out of the building, not wanting to see if Octavius managed to save it before it hit the flames.

*** XXI ***

'Okay, you two' Aaronn said the next morning to Trae and Octavius 'I want you to shake hands, and call it quits.'

'No!' Octavius folded his tentacles across his chest, and turned so his back was facing Trae 'he's hurt my feelings!'

'Your feelings!' Trae yelled 'what about my feelings?!'

'What about your feelings? You don't have any or you wouldn't have killed those people. It's all about me. Me, me, me.'

'I'm surprised you can fit in this room with your ego' Trae said, 'you are the worst thing that I have had to deal with – EVER!'

'Indignity after indignity' Octavius looked at Aaronn 'are you going to let him speak to me like that?'

'You two are behaving like children' Aaronn said as he shuffled some papers in front of him. 'I am tired of having to deal with your antics, Octavius, and your incident reports, Trae. This has got to stop.'

'He started it' Trae said.

'Oh, that's right, blame the guy who's different' said Octavius 'like you always do. I thought you were supposed to care for everyone no matter who they were.'

'That's enough!' Aaronn looked around, as the furniture started to shake 'Now what?' The walls began to vibrate, as a rumble could be felt through the floor, and the table began to shift, and walk forward as the shaking increased.

'Earthquake!' Trae dived under the table.

'Get out of there' Aaronn said as he staggered to the window 'we have never had an earthquake. I can't see why we would have one now.' He looked outside 'Well would you look at that.'

Trae crawled out from under the table, and stood by Aaronn, and Octavius as they looked out of the window. 'Oh, wow!' Trae said, 'look at all the swoop owls, what are they doing?' He watched as what appeared to be thousands of swoop owls, were running down the main road. Cars had stopped as there were so many running through, some jumped on top of the cars, as they ran over them, leaving the cars with dents in them.

'Well,' Admiral Melon spoke behind them, which caused Trae to jump 'there's an old tale that's told around these parts, about the mythical swoop owls, and if they stampede, which they are doing, it is an omen of something terrible that's going to happen.'

'What could possibly happen on an island?' Trae scratched his head as though he were thinking.

'That's why the tale says that something terrible will happen, it doesn't say what' Admiral Melon laughed, and slapped Trae on the back.

'Let's go watch them from outside' Octavius said, 'they're heading for the jetty.' Octavius led the way, with the others following.

They stood on the sidewalk and watched the swoop owls running down the road to the jetty, row after row they ran in unison, in what seemed to be a never-ending sea of owls. 'I've never seen anything like this' Trae said, 'can they swim?'

'I don't think so' Aaronn said, 'but I didn't realise that there were so many that were living here.'

'So, they're going to drown' Trae said, 'how sad.'

'They're an omen of doom' General Melon said, 'I can feel it in my bones.'

'That's probably your arth-' Trae's sentence was cut off by someone yelling for help. A loud deep man's voice kept yelling.

'HELP! Help, I need help. Someone, anyone – HELP!'

They looked around, trying to find who had called for help, but they couldn't see anyone. They looked at each other and shrugged.

'HELP! SAVE ME!'

'Ha, ha, ha' Octavius laughed and pointed up a nearby tree 'Look up there everyone. What are you doing up there, Pain?!'

'THE OWLS, SAVE ME!'

Octavius laughed so much he started to roll around on the ground. 'He's scared of the little birds. I can't believe it, big, tough, Pain is scared of a bird.'

'Pain is scared of the swoop owls, but they're harmless' Trae said as he looked at Pain clinging to the branches. *This is the guy who tries to hurt himself, and he's scared of swoop owls.*

'Pain, get down here!' Aaronn ordered.

'NO, IT'S NOT SAFE!'

'GET DOWN HERE!' Aaronn yelled 'WE'LL PROTECT YOU IF YOU'RE THAT SCARED!'

They watched as Pain tentatively climbed down, and then hid behind Admiral Melon, and held onto him as though he were a shield, as the swoop owls continued to stampede down the road, to the jetty, and into the sea.

'We need to get out of here, sir' Pain said as he stepped backwards to the building behind them, keeping the admiral in front of him, he pulled him along with him till they were inside the building.

'Pain, this is not like you' Admiral Melon said, 'I think you need some exercise to destress.'

Trae shook his head and went back inside after Pain and the admiral had entered to finish up for the day. *Old wives' tales, tough man scared of a little bird, an egotistical, murderous octopus, there's plenty wrong with the island, nothing worse could possibly happen, it was already a nightmare.*

'And I'm telling you nothing bad will happen' Trae said to the receptionist as he yawned as he left the office 'nothing has happened, nothing will happen, it's just a stupid old wives' tale.'

It's been a week already and nothing bad has happened Trae yawned as he walked home *it's going to be an early night for me, I can't believe I'm so tired. I can't believe how stupid people have been this week, they were way more superstitious, avoiding stepping on cracks in the pavement, throwing salt over their shoulder when they spilt it, avoiding ladders, it was a whole new level of crazy. What is going on here?* He unlocked his door and walked in. *Yet here we are a week later, and as I said nothing has happened. Besides all the other stuff.*

*** XXII ***

The sound of a phone ringing woke Trae up. He groaned and looked at the clock. *Two a.m.* He shook his head and picked his mobile up. *Whoa, thirteen missed calls ... I wonder what's happened.* He dialled Aaronn's number. *What's that smell? What's that noise?* Trae put the loudspeaker on and got dressed. *Why is the floor moving?*

'About time!' Aaronn yelled down the phone 'where are you?!'

'I was asleep' Trae yawned 'what's all the noise?'

'We're evacuating the island. Get down here?'

'Evacuation, but why, and where is here?'

'The beach, get down here, there's a volcano that's appeared, and looking to erupt!'

'Vo-vo-volcano' a rush of adrenaline surged through Trae as he realised the danger there could be and finished quickly pulling the rest of his clothes on.

'Just get down here now, there are injuries!' Aaronn disconnected the call.

Trae pushed his way through the crowd of people, who were running to the already crowded beach. *How am I supposed to find Aaronn with all these people? Where do I start?* Trae looked around; the darkness of the night was lit up by the light of the full moon.

'Attention, everybody, don't panic!'

Trae groaned *I know that voice* He looked in the direction of where he heard it. There was Octavius hanging upside down from one of the palm trees, as he spoke into a megaphone.

Trae looked in amazement as the people on hearing Octavius, calmed down, and stopped panicking.

Trae pushed his way through the crowd to where Octavius was hanging, because he knew that was where Aaron, and Sloane probably were. *What's that light?* He looked up into the sky and saw a laser beam doing loops.

'Aha' Octavius pointed his rifle at the light 'you're drunk Rude Dolphin, but finally, I'll get you.'

'He's not drunk' Trae coughed, 'he's probably overcome by the fumes from the volcano.'

'So now you're an expert in reindeerology' Octavius swung around to get a better aim 'just hold still for one moment.'

'Yes' Trae said defeatedly 'I'm an expert in reindeerology, I've been studying.' He went to see Aaronn.

'Got him' Octavius laughed as a shot rang out, and Rude Dolphin fell into the sea.

'About time you showed up' Aaronn said as he listened to his mobile. 'Great' he turned to Sloane 'rescue ships won't be here for four days.'

'Four days!' Trae interrupted 'but when is this volcano going to blow? Although we'll all die very soon anyway, from the ash and fumes.'

'Cheery soul aren't you. Best guestimate is a couple of days' Sloane said 'if we're lucky, could be a couple of hours. Anyone want to bet on how long it takes?'

'We'll die!'

'Stop whining, Trae' Aaronn said. He looked at Sloane 'We really need to talk about your gambling habit, if we get off here.'

'Aaronn!' Pain panted as he ran up 'I know how to save everyone!'

'Fantastic, finally someone who has thought of something, go on.'

'I will throw myself into the volcano and appease the volcano gods.'

'That's your idea' Aaronn stared at Pain.

'What? Are you insane?' Trae spluttered.

'C'mon, Aaronn' Pain insisted 'I want to smell the sulphur and feel the lava rip through my flesh.'

'Pain, you are not going anywhere near the volcano!' Aaronn ordered.

'But Aaronn!'

'No buts, Pain!' Aaronn ordered 'Trae, go find some people to mend.'

Like that will be helpful if we're dead Trae began to wander amongst the crowd, which was easier now that dawn was breaking.

'People!' Octavius yelled through a megaphone as he swung from the tree, and landed on the ground next to Aaronn 'quick, we must make rafts. Grab what you can.'

'Simmer, Brigadier, the boats might be here earlier.'

'Let's see, Aaronn' Octavius pretended to think 'stay here with an active volcano and definitely die, or escape on a wonky raft, and maybe die. You do the maths! I'm going to cut some trees down for them.'

'Aaronn!' Trae ran over to them a short time later 'do you see what these people are doing? They are building rafts, and they don't look too safe. These rafts are not the best. Look at that one, they literally have 4 logs tied in a square with vines, they don't even have a middle.'

'I don't see a better plan, and it's nice to see everyone working together, and the way they're working, they'll be finished in no time. Anyone would think there was an emergency or something.' Aaronn laughed to himself as though he had made a joke.

'There is an emergency' Trae threw his hands up in the air in disgust 'oh, I quit. I've had enough.'

'Trae, you need to simmer down, it's not good for your blood pressure' Sloane said as she joined them 'I'm not a doctor, and even I know that.'

'We have succeeded!' Octavius yelled a few hours later. 'Onwards people … use your hands, use whatever you've made, just row, and row hard, and fast!' He started to herd the islanders onto the rafts that they had made. 'C'mon!' he yelled to Aaronn, Sloane, Trae, Pain and Admiral Melon 'I've saved the last one for us!' He pushed the raft out, 'I made it myself.'

'Why are we going in the opposite direction to everyone else?' asked Trae.

'Because they're going to the mainland, and we're not' Octavius said.

'But, what happened to no one going back to the mainland?'

'Trae, our home is going to blow up, besides who is going to believe them if they talk about me, which they won't.'

'And why won't they talk?' Trae sighed as the tide moved them away from the island. 'I want to go back.'

Octavius laughed 'They know I'll hunt them down and kill them if they do. Now stop whining, or I'll make you row.' He handed Trae a makeshift oar from a thin tree trunk.

'I'm not rowing, you row.'

'What!' Octavius folded two tentacles across his chest 'let's get one thing straight, I'm not rowing, I don't want to get a splinter in my tentacle. Besides, I made the raft, what have you done, ever - except complain.'

'Will you two be quiet?' Aaronn said, 'I'm trying to get a signal.'

Hours later, a thunderous explosion echoed across the sky, which had turned red. They grabbed the vines that tied the trees, that had been used for the raft, as the boat lurched to one side.

'Hang on everyone!' Octavius yelled 'there's a huge wave coming.'

'Get off me!' Aaronn yelled, as Octavius climbed up onto his back, and held on, as it hit. 'Yee haa!' he cried out as the surge sent the boat further along the waves.

'You're insane!' Trae said to Octavius when the waves had settled. *I can't believe we're still alive.*

'Stop picking on me, Trae!' Octavius climbed off Aaronn's back 'You don't hear Aaronn complaining.'

'Would it do any good if I did?' Aaronn stretched 'You're getting heavier, brigadier.' He looked out into the dusk skyline, trying to spot somewhere they could land. Without warning Pain jumped into the ocean. 'Get back in here!' Aaronn yelled as he saw a shark fin cut through the water.

'C'mon little fishy' Pain ignored Aaronn. 'C'mon and take a bite out of me.'

'See, Trae' Octavius gloated 'I'm not the crazy one.'

Pain screamed as the shark bit his hand, and blood filled the water. 'Oh, the pain, I love it, c'mon fishy take another bite, you missed the main part of me.'

'Octavius!'

'On it, Aaronn!' Octavius slipped into the water and swam over to where Pain was thrashing about. He grabbed the shark's tail with his tentacles and held it so it couldn't go any further forward, but just made it swim around in circles.

'Okay, Trae go get Pain' Aaronn threw Trae into the sea.

Trae spluttered as he surfaced. 'Aaronn?'

'Just help him in' Aaronn ordered 'I don't want blood on my uniform.'

'You're getting soft' Admiral Melon said, as he jumped in 'hang on Trae, I'll help you.'

Admiral Melon and Trae pulled Pain back to the raft, then with Sloane, and Aaronn, they helped to pull Pain onto it. 'Okay, Octavius, we've got him' Aaronn yelled, as he watched Trae, rip a piece of his shirt off, and tie a tourniquet around Pain's lower arm.

Octavius surfaced, with the shark in his tentacles. He swung the shark around in a few circles before letting go, sending the shark sailing across the water. Octavius slapped two of his tentacles together. 'And that's how you get rid of sharks' he yelled out to them, as he swam back to the boat, and climbed on board.

'No, Trae' Aaronn said 'it's been a very long couple of days already, just leave it and get some sleep.' Not a sound could be heard as night fell, bar the lapping of waves as they hit the boat.

Oh, what is that noise? Trae yawned as he woke up, *I can't believe I actually fell asleep.* He looked at the seagulls that were flying nearby.

'Ahoy there me mateys!' Octavius pointed 'I spy us some land!'

'Wow, Aaronn, look!' Trae looked in the direction Octavius was pointing 'Land. How long do you think it will take to get there?'

'Depends how fast you swim' Aaronn said.

'What do you mean? I'm not swimming, what about sharks?' Trae looked at the others as they prepared to dive into the water.

'You don't have a choice, Trae' Aaronn laughed 'Octavius has untied the vines. Stay here if you want, but it will sink.'

'Of all the stupid, but why?!' Trae stood on the edge ready to dive in.

'Because I can" Octavius pushed Trae in, and then dived in after the others. 'Beat you to the island' he said as he sank under the waves and headed to the island.

Trae spluttered as he resurfaced and slapped the sea with his hand. *That stupid octopus has got to die.* He started to swim behind the others, as they headed towards the island. *Maybe it won't be so bad. A new island, a new beginning, it's not like it can get any worse. Nope, it's all turning out to be okay.*